Reinventing Mike Lake

By R.W. Jones

Reinventing Mike Lake

Copyright: R.W. Jones

Publisher: Endless String

First Published: June 2012

Second Edition: September 2012

ISBN: 978-0-9856431-1-9

To: Jessica

1

People tend to do pretty drastic things when they come to the conclusion that there is nothing left to fear. I wasn't always like that, and I still may not be like that at all. With her gone, something changed. An emptiness that I never knew possible came through me like a train you never see coming, and I never saw it coming.

At first you don't believe it; nobody ever believes it when it shows up at their front door. From the start it didn't look good. She hung on for almost a year, but from the two month period on, she wasn't herself. At times I accepted it, and other times I denied it. When it finally happened, I denied it.

There were so many dreams we never accomplished. Complacency is a death in itself. We never had kids, because when we decided it was time, we learned it was too late. We never had a house to call our own, instead renting from a family friend at a generous price. The vacations were fun, but not having children or owning a house are two things that we considered failed dreams. We never talked about it, but we both felt it.

The first thing I did was lay there, then I laid some more, and followed that up with more lying. Walking to the bathroom was the extent of my physical activity. I turned on the television, then turned to video games, and eventually started to read. I took myself off the radar screen I had never been on much to begin with.

Nearly a year passed, and I finally started to come around. By "come around" I mean I got out of bed for longer than a few minutes at a time. I started to write again because I felt like that's what I should be doing.

I walked my dog, Bahama, a lot. After close to a year of immobility, we both needed the exercise. Luckily for Bahama she had my parents' daily visits to look forward to for exercise and interaction, but it wasn't enough. As Bahama and I began to slim down, I felt even better, though I suspect the sunlight had as much to do with my turnaround as did losing a few pounds.

Even though a year had gone by, it never dawned on me I was living on my own. In reality I wasn't living at all. My parents brought me food, did my laundry, and cleaned my house. I can't imagine they enjoyed seeing their only son in that situation, but at the time that's the only situation I wanted to be in. They didn't press me to snap out of it. I was free to let my grief go wherever it wanted to go. I knew even in the depths of the darkest parts and feelings of my grief that if things were getting out of control, my parents would have stepped in.

It was the reading that helped more than anything. At first, nothing inspired me, but then I started reading stories about people who had taken chances. The stories about college kids hiking through European countries were all well and good, but I was most interested in the adventures of those down and out like me. The stories about people who set out with little – or better yet – no plans stirred something inside me the most. I began getting goosebumps when I read their stories, showing more life than I had in months. I'm sure some of the stories were fabricated, but as a former storyteller I hardly cared. More importantly, something inside me was stirring.

Even at my happiest times, I've always had a nagging feeling that I was missing something. I had never taken my great adventure, and from the comment boxes of the stories I was reading online, I wasn't the only one. Most comments read something like the following: "I enjoy your story so much and wish I could do something like it, but X, Y, and Z has kept me from doing so." X, Y, and even Z were sometimes valid points, but more often than not they seemed like an excuse or fear of the unknown. As someone who never lived farther away than ten minutes from my parents, I could relate. During my year of sulking, my greatest adventure was walking one of the small loop trails that surrounded our house.

But it was on those fifteen-minute walks that I began fantasizing about a different kind of life, one with no restraints, rhyme, or reason. I often pictured Bahama and me just continuing our walk past the confines of the trail, the neighborhood, the city, the state, and beyond. In those walking daydreams I imagined I wouldn't tell anyone, I would just leave. But I always had the feeling that I wouldn't be able to do it like that. Mainly, I wouldn't want to worry my family and friends. I thought they would think I had done something drastic. Looking back and remembering my less than fragile state of mind during this time, I can't say I would have blamed them for thinking the worst had I just disappeared. I'm glad that I kept my parents' feelings in consideration even while feeling my lowest. Still the fantasies continued, and eventually they became all-consuming.

From the time I was really young – maybe middle school – I always had an issue with what society deemed normal. The routine of everyone doing the same thing every day was always mind boggling to me. By "the same," I mean the 9 to 5, going to bed at the same time, going to college to get that 9 to 5, eating at the same time every day. I didn't know how to put it into words back then, and I still don't know how to for the most part, but I just knew that I wanted to eat when I was hungry, sleep when I was tired, and work when I wanted to work. I didn't want a clock on the wall to dictate what I did. This way of thinking may suggest that I was a nightmare for teachers and to my parents, but I wasn't. Like so much else, I usually kept these thoughts in my head and fell in line with everyone else. Other than becoming a writer, I did very little in my life to back up the thoughts I thought of so much during my life.

I don't remember what particular story I read that brought me over the edge, but one night I knew I was going to do it. I can only imagine my parents' surprise when exactly one year after the day my wife died I left a note on my kitchen table that read:

"Dear Mom and Dad,

Bahama and I went on a little longer walk than usual. We will call when we get to where we are going.

Love,
Us"

2

My parents, being the insightful people they are, surely noticed that my SUV was missing from the garage, so they knew in short order that our walk was actually a drive. Regardless, I am sure that my mode of transportation was hardly their main concern when they noticed Bahama and I had left the house in quick fashion. While the topic of suicide had never been discussed between my parents and me, I knew my parents were concerned that was a route I could pursue.

One night after dinner at their house during my year of grieving, I went into my old room, now the den, intending to check my e-mail. Instead I was greeted with a Google web search one of my parents, presumably my mother, had recently done. In the search box was "what to do if you expect someone could commit suicide." She had 7,840,000 websites to help her answer that question, according to the search result, yet the issue had never come up between us. Forgetting about my e-mail, I walked out of the room, kissed my mom goodnight, and told her, "Don't worry; I would never do that to you." She looked at me, and smiled. Despite this moment – one I thought had cleared up any concern my mother may have – I knew it would be in the best interest of everyone if I called her soon and let her know I was okay. I wanted to wait until I had an idea of exactly what I was doing before I called them.

About the only thing I knew was that the car was heading south. Bahama's 20-pound frame was sitting on the console between the driver and passenger side seats, performing her duties as co-pilot. I thought to ask her where we were going. The last time I had this profile view of Bahama, my wife was right on the other side. I knew that leaving the house could bring a whirlwind of emotions with it, but I still wasn't prepared for the thoughts every memory could elicit.

At the same time we hit the state line of North Carolina, I instantly remembered that I wasn't the only one in my family that had endured a major period of pain and grieving. Just eight months ago, my sister Chloe saw her own marriage end suddenly. Unfortunately, I lost count on the number of years Chloe and her husband Richard had been married because my sister and I had been estranged for years, mostly because of Richard. After I heard the news of their divorce, I called Chloe offering an apology, but she simply said, "It's what you all wanted anyway." She then hung up the receiver with a thud.

I learned shortly after that phone call that the last thing Richard has ever said to Chloe and their 6-year old daughter Cassidy was, "I hope I never see you two sluts again." In the months since, Richard had made no attempt to see his daughter. My mom heard Richard was living on a friend's couch in Tennessee, but she wasn't really sure. Being waist deep in my own grieving, I didn't think to offer condolences to Chloe. Plus, she was right, it is what we wanted, but we didn't want it to happen that way. My mom's plate was full dealing with both of our mourning periods while knowing that her son and daughter didn't talk to each other.

Despite having many uncles, aunts, and cousins living within close proximity of each other, our main family consisted of only my parents and my sister, about four years older than me. We grew up without the constant bickering between siblings that I had seen in nearly all my friends. When we had problems in school – tough tests, tough teachers, or tough situations with boyfriends and girlfriends – we always came to each other. Though we would never admit it at the time, we were best friends. When she met Richard while in college, things changed between us.

Richard was an alcoholic and despite being charming at times, his inability to control his drinking, and in turn, his temper, was concerning to our family. We weren't friends at all, but we went to the same small college, so our paths crossed frequently at bars and house or dorm parties. Partying and college of course go hand and hand for many, including myself, but it was evident his drinking was out of control, even at a young age. Richard came from a family of hard drinkers, and because of this he had been advised by concerned family members that he should slow down his drinking, or better yet, quit altogether. But like a child you repeatedly tell not to touch something, the temptation, and perhaps the genetic inclination, was too much.

I always held out hope that Richard would slow down, but had my doubts. Chloe assured us he was just "being a college kid," but deep down I suspect she knew his drinking was more than that. Sure enough, after college he was drinking even more. The problem now was that he was married to my sister. Even on the day of their wedding I smelled liquor on his breath, even after their reverend, the same reverend that had married my parents 26 years prior, politely asked no one in the wedding party, which I also presumed included the groom, to not drink on the day of the wedding until after the ceremony. You didn't need to smell it on his breath to know he had been drinking; his eyes had given it away.

After the wedding, my sister and I grew farther apart, both by relationship and distance, after they moved to North Carolina. My sister was a dental assistant, and attributed the move to her job, but in reality I believe she was trying to separate herself from the constant arguments regarding her husband and our family. She had hoped of going to dental school, but when the time came to make the decision, she opted not to go. My parents said this was because Richard said it wasn't necessary because he would make a lot of money. He, of course, was saying these things when he was jobless, a title he held for most of their relationship. Because Chloe didn't go to dental school, a goal she had spoke about for years; it further diminished her relationship with our parents. It wasn't that my parents had been forcing her to go to dental school; they just knew in their hearts that she wasn't going largely because of Richard.

Over time we stopped calling each other. During the last few years I had only seen her once, at my wife's funeral, but we hardly spoke, though I hardly spoke to anyone that day, or in the following year. After Richard left, I wasn't quick to offer condolences when she was surely going through one of the hardest times of her life. My parents had gone down to North Carolina occasionally after the divorce to help her get back on her feet, but I had never gone on any of those trips. Instead of being thankful my parents were going down to help my sister out, I remember being upset that they were leaving me during my time of mourning. I never stopped to consider the position my parents were in: dealing with mourning children.

When I got in my SUV that morning, I'd be lying if I said it was with the goal to visit my sister. The "Welcome to North Carolina" sign and the resulting thought process was responsible for that. Still I physically had to make the decision if I was going to visit her or not. I'm sure she would be surprised, to say the least, to see me. I still had 60 miles to mull my decision.

As my sister's exit grew closer, my heartbeat grew faster. I had decided what I was going to do. I pulled out my cell phone to call my parents. My mom answered before the line even rang on my end.

"Where are you?" she asked, worried.

"I'm getting ready to go see Chloe," I replied. "I remember the city, but can't remember the address." Truth is – I never knew it.

After a pause on the other end of the line in which I could tell my mom was processing this information, she said with what sounded like a smile, "I'll be right back, it's in my address book." I knew she was happy, as we always had an understanding that didn't involve many words.

3

I parked just on the edge of her long circular driveway, about as far away as I could be from her house while still on her property. In my mind this gave me a chance to leave unnoticed if I were to change my mind before I got up to the door. I quickly realized this wouldn't be an option. About five seconds after I put the car into park I could see through the dusk that the front door had opened.

"Who's there?!" yelled a man's voice I didn't recognize, causing Bahama to turn her head questionably.

"Mike, Chloe's sister – I mean – brother," I yelled back, nervous of the voice I couldn't see. I waited for a response for a few seconds. When none came, I begrudgingly headed to the door.

The screen door was shut, but the front door remained opened. As soon as I reached the top step Chloe appeared, with her daughter Cassidy in tow. I wasn't sure if our mother had called Chloe or not, but given the welcoming I got from her man friend, I guessed the answer was no.

Because of Bahama's black and brown fur and the darkening sky, she was tough to see, but as soon as Cassidy saw Bahama she squealed, "OHHHH! A PUPPY! Can I play with it?" looking excitedly between her mom and my best friend. While Bahama was far from a puppy, coming in at around seven years old, she still acted like one when meeting a new friend.

"Yes, go ahead take her out back. We should have a tennis ball," replied Chloe, but Cassidy and Bahama were through the back door before the sentence was finished.

Chloe didn't invite me in verbally, but turned around and headed back into the center of the house, leaving the front door open behind her. I took this as an invite, and headed in.

In the living room, Chloe was just turning off the television, and sat down on one end of a large sectional couch. I sat down on the opposite side.

"If you're busy, I can leave and come back another time," I said while motioning with my head where I guessed her visitor was, though I really had no clue.

"Oh, that's Mr. Fields, my neighbor. He was fixing my water heater for me. He owns the company that installed it."

"Well, he didn't seem too happy to see me."

"He's just been helping me out some since Richard left. Being our closest neighbor he heard a lot of what was going on over here. He also has a daughter my age, so I guess it comes natural to him to protect me a bit." When she mentioned the part about Richard leaving she glanced in my direction to see my reaction. I wasn't sure how I was supposed to react. I followed up with what I thought was a safe question. I was wrong.

"How are things anyway? How is your daughter dealing with everything?"

She made a snorting sound under her breath and then let me have it, which I had sort of been expecting, saying, "You don't even know her name do you?"

I did.

"Did you drive down here yourself just to make sure he was gone?"

I hadn't.

"I know you guys didn't like him, but he was

11

my husband and I loved him," she said, fighting back tears.

I didn't know what to say. I hadn't really known what to say to her for the last few years, so this was nothing new, except now I was in the same room as her. I said the first thing that came to my mind.

"Thank you for coming to the funeral. I'm sorry I wasn't here more for you in your time of need."

I could tell anger was still boiling up in her, which reminded me of her when we were kids. Right before you thought she was going to explode into a fit of screaming rage she always began to cry. With that thought, she began to cry.

On cue, my friend Mr. Fields walked into the room, two foot wrench in hand. He had looked big standing in the doorway at dusk, now just a few feet away I could see he was well over six feet tall and upwards of 300 pounds. At just under six feet tall and 185 pounds, and not having a wrench handy, I didn't like my chances. After glaring at me, he asked Chloe, "Do you want me to get rid of this guy?"

In my mind I begged for Chloe to say no, as I had already thought of about eight different ways how that wrench could be involved in the getting-rid process that Mr. Fields had planned for me.

Chloe looked up, the sobbing beginning to subside and said, "No, Mr. Fields, I'm fine. This is my brother, he came down from Virginia to get to know his niece and catch up a little." I hadn't realized that's what I was doing there, but any answer that didn't involve a wrench and my body was fine with me.

Mr. Fields looked at me one more time then back at my sister, this time with a little less of a scowl, and said, "The water heater should be fine now. If it acts up, let me know. Hope to see you over at our place

Tuesday. Mrs. Fields is making her famous tuna casserole Tuesday night." As Mr. Fields left, Chloe asked me how I like my ice cream. Feeling that I had waited way too long to be sarcastic, I replied, "Cold."

4

Cassidy and Bahama, tennis ball in her mouth, came inside to join us for ice cream. Cassidy had chocolate, while Bahama had a sizable scoop of vanilla. Both Cassidy and Bahama ate their ice cream breathlessly, both looking like they could fall asleep any minute after what must have been a spirited game of fetch. After finishing hers, Bahama laid on her side on the cool floor. After tiring of the floor, she trotted into the living room and popped up on the sectional couch. Chloe told me that I better hope it's as comfortable to me as it looked for Bahama because that would be my bed too for the duration of my stay.

Over the ice cream, I had been mentally preparing for a long conversation I predicted would last deep into the night, but after fighting with Cassidy to bathe and get her into bed, Chloe told me she was exhausted and would be going to bed herself. She told me I would find the proper linens in the hallway closet and gave me the customary run down of how to turn on the shower.

I laid awake for a few hours, wanting to sleep, but instead watching the same episode of *SportsCenter* twice, and finally falling asleep to a documentary of past NBA champions on ESPN Classic. All and all a typical night for me over the last year, only now I was on my sister's couch and about 200 miles from home with no idea what tomorrow would bring.

The next morning I was awakened by the sound of Cassidy's voice, "Uncle Mike, wake up, wake up!" I had guessed by my body's weariness that it was early, maybe even still in the single digit a.m. hours. During my grieving I had become adept at waking up in the single digit hours too, only the clock read "p.m."

"Hey sweetie, good morning," I grunted, while trying to sound as nice as I possibly could, while reaching for my cell phone. 6:46 a.m. Ugh.

Cassidy said, "What's for breakfast? Mom said you'd make me breakfast! I'm starrrrving," drawing out the word starving for emphasis.

I said, "How about some ice cream?"

Cassidy smiled brightly, but then seeming to remember her mom wouldn't approve, changed to a frown and replied, "Mommy wouldn't let me do that."

I got up, while Bahama snoozed away, and sleepily headed for the kitchen. Turning on the bright lights caused me to cringe, but I kept on a happy face for my "starrrrving" niece. I was no chef, but I was able to make the basics, like toast and eggs. I made these as quickly as I could before Cassidy asked for something more complex, like pancakes.

After eating, I cleaned the dishes and put them in the dishwasher. Despite making just toast and eggs I had managed to mess up the once-clean kitchen beyond recognition. As I was finishing up, Chloe came down the stairs in a bathrobe that I'm fairly sure she wouldn't have worn if there was a man in her house other than her brother.

"Sexy," I said to her, when she came around the corner.

She put up the pointer, middle, and ring fingers of her right hand and said, "read between the lines," smiling. I was happy to see our back and forth was coming back like we hadn't missed a step – or years.

Luckily Cassidy had missed the bird shot by her mother because she had already moved on to the couch to try to wake up Bahama. I didn't think she had much of a chance, but before I knew it I heard the two of them running up and down the hallway.

Chloe sat down, cup of coffee in hand.

"So, what are you doing?" she asked.

"Eating breakfast," I replied. Before she could flip another bird in my direction, I continued.

"You know, I don't really know what I'm doing. I stayed in the house for a year straight for the most part, other than taking Bahama out for a walk every now and then. I know I've always been a bit anti-social, but this, this doing nothing, has been a new experience for me. I realized the only way I was going to heal was by doing something. Anything."

I hadn't expected to be talking about myself so seriously first thing in the morning, but because I had thought we were going to have this conversation last night I was prepared.

Chloe stared at me for a few seconds with an amused look on her face, thinking.

"Well, you are more than welcome to stay here until you figure out what exactly it is you want to do," then paused before saying, "Plus Cass likes your mutt there."

I wasn't shocked by her invitation, but it did surprise me. Without saying it, I think this was her way of extending an olive branch, although I should have been the one to extend it long ago. Still, this was a step in the right direction.

"As long as Mr. Fields says it's okay," I responded.

For six nights I reconnected with my sister, and connected with the niece I never knew. I watched as she and Bahama bonded. To my surprise, Bahama even slept in Cassidy's bed for the rest of the time we were there. I was beginning to think that it would be hard for Cassidy – and probably even Bahama – when it was time for me to leave to wherever I was going next.

The thought had crossed my mind that I could leave Bahama with Cassidy until I got back but knew that wouldn't work for me. Bahama had been by my side, almost 100 percent, for the last seven years, and I always envisioned her by my side when I first had fantasies of wanting to get away. So, I came up with the second best idea.

"Hey Sis," I started, shortly after finishing up dinner one night and after Cassidy and Bahama had gone out back for another round of fetch. "Cassidy has bonded with Bahama pretty well since we've been here and I feel bad that I'm leaving in a couple of days." I paused to see if she knew where I was going. By the skeptical look on her face, she did.

"I was wondering if I – I mean we – could get her a dog of her own, maybe tomorrow, before I leave."

Chloe thought for a moment, and explained to me how it was really hard for her to imagine bringing a puppy into the house when she was already working full-time as a legal secretary and was considering getting a second job. Additionally, she had no help around the house, other than Mr. Fields, so she really had no desire to go through the tasks of housetraining a dog and dealing with all the other things a young puppy generally included. So, again, I thought of the next best thing.

"How about we get her a dog that's a bit older, maybe a couple years old, and you won't have to deal with all of the house training? It's not a human friend, but I think Cassidy would love the companionship. I know I do."

Chloe agreed reluctantly saying "I have to admit, she has really come out of a shell since you've been here. Lately it's been all I could do to get her to go outside."

She had said since "I" had been here, and even though that made me feel like a proud uncle, I knew she really meant since "Bahama" has been here. Still, I was happy "we" could help. She hesitated before saying, "We'll surprise her tomorrow." Then she added, "I'll send you the vet bills."

5

I have never had the experience of taking a child to Disney World, but I imagine an SPCA is a close alternative. Especially after you tell her she can have her pick of the litter, so to speak. To an adult the SPCA resembles a prison. The sad commercials you see while flipping through the channels late at night don't help either.

At first she ran through the hallways of the SPCA scaring most of the dogs, while some of the other ones scared her. During all this her mother was trying to explain to her that we need to make sure she doesn't pick a dog that is too big, and that it has to be a bit older. She explained to Cassidy that by picking one that was a little older she'd be doing a good thing because everyone else would be picking the puppies, so they would be sure to have a good home. I didn't want to see Cassidy have to turn down a puppy she really liked, but luckily the puppies were in a separate section of the facility and Cassidy never asked about them, so we were never faced with that decision. The only thing I added was that we also wanted to make sure the new doggy got along with Bahama since we would be visiting often. Bahama was currently in a "meet and greet" room in the front of the building garnering the attention of a handful of volunteers. While all the humans involved in the decision of bringing a new dog home for Cassidy held an important say, Bahama held the biggest. Her reaction to the potential new addition would make or break the deal.

The first dog Cassidy took outside was a Chihuahua named Killer that didn't stop barking from the time we took him out of his run with the help of a reluctant volunteer. Chloe shot me a look that said, "If she picks this dog, I will never forgive you." Unfortunately for the Chihuahua mix, Cassidy was pretty fearful of the dog once she got a closer look, so Killer's outside portion of the talent show didn't even make it to the Bahama part of the program. Cassidy said something to her mom about being afraid of the dog, and Chloe, trying her best not to look to thankful, whisked the dog back to his run.

The second dog, who had yet to be given a name from the staff, had potential right from the start. We took the beagle-mix to the side of the building where they had a fenced in section. I then walked back inside to get Bahama to see if we would be getting her approval. Cassidy, Chloe, and I all knew that the decision rested solely in her paws.

When I walked back to the yard I saw Cassidy and the no-named pup playing with a rope, with the beagle-mix taking it easy on her end of the toy. I took it as a good thing that the dog knew her own strength when playing with a child as small as Cassidy.

When Bahama saw the beagle, her tail beat against my leg. Her fur didn't stick up, so I knew she wasn't scared, like how I had seen her react around some of the dogs in my neighborhood. Bahama was so excited to go play with Cassidy and the new dog that I thought there was a chance she'd break the leash on our way over to them. The commotion got the attention of the beagle-mix, so the volunteer met us halfway, trying to not lose hold of the leash. After preliminary introductions, they both ran back towards Cassidy, with what can only be described as doggy smiles.

"So does Mommy have any say in your new addition's name?" I asked Chloe.

"No, I'm going to let Cassidy name her. Isn't that exciting?"

After paperwork that took an hour, and waiting for a long line of volunteers to say goodbye to the no-named beagle they had fallen in love with, we headed back to Chloe's place. I didn't have much time to get to know the newest member of the family because there was food, leashes, and a crate to be bought. I went to the pet store solo, and the entire trip took about an hour. When I returned to the house the no-named beagle-mix was still a no-named beagle-mix.

"She wants to name it 'Uncle Mike'," Chloe reported as I walked back into the house with an armful of bags.

Holding back laughter, but feeling flattered, I dropped the bags on the kitchen table and said, "I'm not sure she would appreciate that," emphasizing the word "she," as in the sex of the dog.

"I told her she'd have to change it, she's thinking about it now. The whole clan is in the yard playing."

Around the dinner table that night, our feet surrounded by worn out doggies, Chloe asked Cassidy if she had come up with a name.

"Ummmmmm, how 'bout Bahama?" she asked, causing Bahama to perk her head off the floor, hoping for a table scrap.

"Well that's her name, how about something else?" her mom asked her, while pointing to my confused dog.

"Okayyyyyy, how about Pink," which I guessed was her favorite color based on the color scheme of her bedroom and most of her clothes.

"What about Pinky?" her mom suggested. She later told me she suggested this name because it flowed off the tongue better. I mentally tested her theory in my head – "Here Pink, Pink, Pink" versus

"Here Pinky, Pinky, Pinky." She had a point.

Throughout all of this the beagle kept an eye on her, and tilted her head every time someone mentioned the name Pinky.

"I think she likes it" I said around the same time Cassidy ran out of the living room with Pinky and Bahama in tow yelling "Pinky" over and over.

"I guess that's that," said Chloe.

And, that was that.

6

I left my sister's house the next morning with plans to see her again, though I made no promises on when, as I didn't know how long this trip would last. I did know that I wanted to see Cassidy grow up. Knowing I couldn't replace the time I already missed watching her grow up was upsetting, but a lot of things were upsetting for me during that time frame. Cassidy seemed pretty forgiving, as kids often are, and I left her house thinking that was good enough for me. She did want to name her dog after me, after all.

Getting back in the car, I really had no clue where I was heading, with the exception of finding myself heading south again. Being in my sister's house in North Carolina was the farthest south I had been since I was a teenager during family vacations, so everywhere I traveled was like new to me. This was just as well.

I started the day on 77-South and then picked up 95-South when 77 forked towards Columbia, South Carolina. I only got out of the car a couple of times for bathroom breaks for Bahama and me.

I was hoping getting back in the car wouldn't cause me to have the same feelings of anxiety as when I first started the trip, but I was wrong. When I was with Chloe and Cassidy I had my mind occupied most of the time, but the quiet of the road caused my mind to scream with doubt. A part of me was doing exactly what I wanted to, which was to just get away from it all, but I was learning it was hard to get away from yourself. Another part questioned everything I was doing. Every mile in the car made it easier to enjoy the trip for what it was, but those early mornings, especially after leaving a place I had been for a little bit, were particularly hard.

I realized I had missed a few opportunities to cut just an hour or two east and be at a beach, and I admitted to myself that that sounded like a nice destination. It was now in the middle of summer, so the beach would be filled to capacity and would make for a good scene.

It was also somewhat surprising I didn't head straight for a beach because I had always felt at peace being there. Unfortunately, I hadn't spent nearly enough time at one to figure out if it was the beach that was giving me that inner peaceful feeling. I had surmised that it was the separation of the things upsetting me that gave me peace while I was at a beach, however brief. Would I feel the same on a mountaintop ski lodge, a farm in the middle of nowhere, or on the moon, as I did on the beach? All I knew was that I intended to do a lot of exploring about how I felt at different locations on this trip. I never did make it to the moon.

As I crossed into Georgia I was reminded of my big rig driving uncle, Tom, who used to tell me about his travels at family reunions. When I was a child, and to a degree even as an adult, I'd always been interested in those stories. I always enjoyed getting a glimpse of the outside world through Tom's colorful storytelling abilities.

My uncle is a large man, standing about 6'6" and at least 325 pounds. One of his favorite subjects to talk about, predictably, is food. He often speaks of steak in Texas, jambalaya in New Orleans, and pizza in New York City. His favorite food however is pork barbeque, and spoke a few times of a "shack of a place" in Brunswick, Georgia that served "the best pork ever." High claims for a man who has perhaps eaten pork barbeque in more states than any other man both past and present.

I couldn't remember what the name of the restaurant was, but I did remember him describing Brunswick as, "if you blink, you'll miss it," so I figured if I kept my eyes open once I took the exit I would find it. It has been many years since my uncle first started telling me his food stories, so Brunswick had grown a little bit, but more or less his description was accurate. Less than a mile off the exit I saw smoke coming from a chimney at the Georgia Pig Shack about 100 yards off the main road.

When I saw the name of the place I instantly remembered a story he told me. He said that his trucker buddies just called it "GA Pig Shack," saying "Gah" instead of "Georgia". Tom said because you sound like a baby when you say "gah" it became known as the "Baby Pig" to them. Quite the history, I thought, for a place that looked like it may fall apart with the first strong wind.

I don't think it would have been out of the realm of possibility to think that this was now an abandoned building. It had the appearance of an old home with an owner who refused to sell even as the rest of the world built around it. However, even from across the road, Bahama's nose perked up and, shortly after, I noticed the sweet-smelling pork going through our air vents.

The front steps creaked as I walked onto a porch that went the distance of the front of the building. A few people were scattered on rocking chairs, smoking cigarettes or pipes. As I went inside one of the smokers, a woman in her 50's followed me in and went behind the counter. I ordered three sandwiches, two for me, and one for Bahama, and a large sweet tea.

The woman washed her hands for about a total of two seconds before preparing my food, which I suppose was better than nothing. It's my guess that she wouldn't have even done that if a health inspector hadn't been by in the last couple of weeks.

Her cleanliness, or lack thereof, reminded me of a day when I worked at a pizza joint during college. We were honestly a pretty clean establishment, but one day my boss told me that a health inspector was coming by and we would have to wash our hands, with soap and water, between every pizza we took out of the oven and placed in the box. Thankfully they came during a mid-week afternoon, one of the slower times, but I still remember my hands being raw after my shift was up. The woman taking my order was washing her hands as if the inspector had been gone for at least a few days, and in a few more customers, they would be lucky if she gave her hands a wipe on her greasy jeans.

While I waited for my order, I got a chance to look around the steamy restaurant that featured zero air-conditioning. To my surprise many celebrities had enjoyed the eatery, including the late Dale Earnhardt, his son Junior, and George W. Bush. Each of those three men, and a few others, had signed an autograph picture of themselves, adding a note about how good the food was. I chuckled to myself making a joke inside my head saying, "Of course they wrote they liked the food, they were probably no more than a few feet away from a man wielding a huge hatchet while cooking up the next batch of pork."

Just as I was done laughing at my own joke, they called my order. It was actually cooler outside than inside, and I wanted to get Bahama out of the car, so I looked for a spot to eat outside. About 50 yards in front of the building I noticed a few lawn chairs, so after scooping Bahama out of the car, I planted myself out in the field, and dug into my first sandwich.

I don't have the meat-eating resume that my uncle has, but it truly was the best barbeque I ever had. Between my first and second sandwich, I threw Bahama her sandwich, and without chewing, it was gone in two seconds. I was so engrossed in my sandwich that I didn't realize the imminent thunderstorm approaching. Around my last bite the skies opened up, and I was drenched in a few seconds. Bahama, who doesn't mind the rain, continued staring at me in hopes of the last bite. Anxious to get out of the rain, I made her dream come true, tossing the soggy bite into her waiting jaws. After running to the porch to throw away my trash, I ran to the car, Bahama enjoying the excitement every step of the way.

My happy stomach must have caused me to doze off for a few minutes, because when I woke up the rain had all but stopped. A quick view of my GPS showed me that we were just over an hour away from Florida. It was still only late afternoon, and I felt fine thanks to my unplanned nap, so I thought heading into Florida was as good of a plan as any. Bahama gave a nodding approval, and we were off.

7

Apparently I had too much sweet tea at the "Baby Pig," because by the time I hit Jacksonville, right over the state line, I had to stop at the first rest area. Bahama enjoys every stop of the car, whether you've been driving eight hours, or if you are in a traffic jam. Each stop is a potential new adventure for her, not to mention a new place to pee. This stop led to an adventure, but it was for me, not her.

By habit, every time I get in and out of the car I check for my wallet, usually secure in my left front pocket. Not this time. After a frantic look inside the car for close to 20 minutes I realized I had lost it. I had a "last time you saw it moment" and was back in line at the GA Pig Shack. I may have left it on the counter, but I hadn't pulled that move off in years, with the last time featuring me being drunk at a bar in college. That time I had maybe a few dollars in it, this time I had a few hundred dollars, plus credit cards and my social security card, but – most importantly – a picture of my wife and I from our first year in college. I found the number to the "Baby Pig" after an internet search on my phone.

It was already a few minutes after seven, and they were only open to eight, so I knew I would have to hurry if I did indeed leave my wallet there. A woman who answered the phone named Karen said she hadn't seen a wallet, but remembered me running for my car from the field when it started pouring. I took this as she remembered making fun of me when it started pouring, but it all but came back to me that the wallet probably popped out when I was running through the field. I didn't make my obligatory wallet check at that point because I was just so happy to be back in the car and promptly dozed off.

When I got back to the restaurant a few minutes after closing time, it was raining again, but not nearly as bad. I was happy to see that a few customers were still in the restaurant when I entered, so I didn't have a guilty feeling that they had waited for me to come back, though I'm not entirely sure they would have waited for me.

A few of the employees were sitting at one of the indoor picnic tables, and eye-balled me inquisitively as I walked through the door. It didn't occur to me at the time that I was dripping wet, and was weary from a day of driving and thinking my wallet, and more importantly my picture with my wife, was missing.

"Is Karen here?" I asked.

"Who's asking?" asked one of the women sitting down, in a gruffer tone than I was expecting.

"Um, well" I stuttered slightly off put, "I lost my wallet..."

"Ohhhh," said the woman who just asked me who's asking. "I'm Karen, I got your wallet right here."

Karen got up and went to the other side of the counter and handed me my drenched wallet, minus three hundred dollars, but credit cards, social security card, and thankfully the picture of my wife and I, still intact. "Someone found it in the field and brought it inside not long after you called."

That "someone" I thought was most likely "Karen" but if you got a look at some of the men and woman she was sitting with at that table behind me, all still staring at me, you probably wouldn't have questioned the missing money either. I also remember having the thought that many of these employees wield cleavers for a living, so I quickly thanked her, and walked back outside, to freedom.

Later on in the trip, when I wasn't so upset about losing the money, realizing it was my own stupidity, I began to appreciate the culture of that part of the country. In the north, and where I live in Virginia is absolutely considered the north when you are in Georgia, everyone in the building would have pointed to "Karen" when I asked where she was. I don't think that the people revealing who "Karen" was would do it with bad intentions, but when you find yourself in the position of "Karen" and some unsavory looking character was looking for you, you certainly hope everyone wouldn't point you out. In the south, there is a sense of privacy, and it seems the residents there, at least the ones that work in the GA Pig Shack in Brunswick, protect each other a little better than their brethren up north.

Back in the car, wallet in place, I weighed my options. Thankfully the money lost wouldn't set me back that much but I still cursed myself for carrying that much on me to begin with, especially considering that my debit card did the same as the cash I had just lost. At that point more than ever, the feelings in the back of my head got louder, constantly asking me, "What is it you hope to accomplish with this trip?" All I had accomplished so far while I was along on the trip was being irresponsible with my valuables and putting my identity at risk.

I considered driving back to Florida because it was only 8 p.m., but I had been driving about ten hours, including backtracking. After my wife died, I am not sure I drove ten hours the entire year. For the first four months I was only a passenger, as my parents came occasionally to pick me up for dinner at their house. Then when I started feeling a bit better, or at least doing a bit more, I would drive to the library, and maybe to the video store, but both of these were just a couple miles from my house. After I purchased the movie streaming service through my video game system, I cut my already meager driving time in half.

Here I was in Brunswick. There was a Comfort Inn across the street, which seemed promising, so I crossed the road, only to see the telltale signs of construction. As I was about to leave the lot, I did see a hand written note written on big letters on the front door that read, "Excuse the dust, but we are open!"

I was able to secure a room for what I thought was an obscene $89.99 a night for this part of the country, but the front desk told me that the Emerald Princess II, a gambling boat that can operate once it hits international waters, had just reopened after a lengthy renovation, so the rooms were about twice the price they usually were to house the itchy gamblers.

I now had information for the next time I found myself in Brunswick, GA. I could eat pork and gamble.

8

The next morning I woke up around 7 a.m. and was starving because I hadn't eaten since my soggy sandwich early in the previous evening. I knew pretty clearly that the "Shack" wouldn't be open that soon, but still I held out hope that they had a pork pancake special. Even before the ritual morning bathroom call, I wandered over to the window and peaked out just to confirm my thoughts. Closed.

With no real reason to stay at a motel in Brunswick for any longer than one absolutely must, I threw myself, Bahama, and our belongings back in the car after a quick shower and a quicker walk. I gave the Pig one last longing look, and got back on the highway heading to Florida, wallet in place.

A couple of exits down the interstate I had found some golden arches to suppress my hunger for the time being. It was around my second bite of this waffle, sausage, egg, and cheese contraption that I began thinking about my health so far on this trip. I had never been a health nut but I knew enough to know combining hours of driving with pork and red meat meal after meal wasn't the greatest of ideas. As many vacationers know, it's really hard to maintain a healthy diet for a week or two. I was planning on being out for a lot longer than a week or two.

As I passed the Jacksonville rest area where I had discovered I was missing my wallet, I instinctively reached into my pocket. It was still there. Good, we will now be conquering new land, I thought. Well, not entirely new land, as I had been in Florida a few times, mostly in my youth, visiting the mouse with big ears and his fun land.

I also have an uncle and aunt that live in a little beach resort called Treasure Island, not far from Tampa. It had been a couple years since I had talked to them, in fact I had never met his new wife, but I knew if I visited them they would still welcome me with open arms. My uncle is the most laid-back person I have ever met.

Uncle Howard, my father's brother, is the black sheep of our family. Most of my family lives within an hour of each other, but from the time my uncle could drive he was hardly ever that close to family again. My uncle has a way of life that I think more people should adopt. He's a permanent vacationer. He lives in places that most of us only visit once or twice a year and think of as a getaway. Our getaways are his homes.

I can't recall all the places he has lived but I do know he's lived on both coasts in Florida, a lot of the coastal cities in California, and even got married to his second wife in Jamaica. He and his first wife remain friends from what I've heard, but the constant moving during the marriage was getting to her, so they agreed, with literally no hard feelings, to separate.

His second wife, Gail, is a bit more of a trooper, and seems to enjoy going along for the ride. Knowing she will never live in an undesirable destination, it's hard to blame her.

I knew that if I was going to be spending any amount of time with Uncle Howard that the idea I had of trying to eat healthy would be on hold. The main reason my uncle eats poorly, I suspect, is because he's a stoner. I don't think he does any other drugs, except drinking occasionally, but I was aware he was a stoner before I even knew what being a stoner entailed. If I had to guess, over the course of my life I have spent maybe 40 to 50 total days in his presence. Of all those meals we shared I can't remember a time we ate a home cooked meal together. Unless toast counts as a home cooked meal – he does put peanut butter on it after all. He once told me that he doesn't eat poorly because he's a stoner. That's what rookie stoners do. He told me he eats the way he does because that's what he prefers to eat. I believe him, but you can be the judge on that.

In each city he's lived in he has a favorite sub, pizza, barbeque, Chinese, and Italian place. What's remarkable is that my uncle is so friendly that I would suspect he gets about half of these carry-out meals for free. It could be that he is very generous, especially with money. Once, when he was living in another beach town in Florida called Vero Beach, I was with him as we went by four of his favorite eateries and dropped a bottle of Patron off to each of their owners.

Because of his generosity, and his never asking for anything in return, the owners all love him and practically throw food at him. When we arrived back to his house after our Patron run, we could barely stuff ourselves through his doorway, holding two pizzas, a bag of Chinese food, my uncle's favorite homemade tortilla chips with three kinds of salsa, and a massive heap of spaghetti featuring what must have been ten pounds of meatballs. It would make sense to expect that my uncle weighs about 500 pounds, but he is actually in pretty good shape because he prefers to live in cities where he can walk everywhere.

Once I passed Jacksonville I knew from my GPS I was about three and a half hours to Treasure Island. I was beginning to get nervous about just showing up unannounced. Still, I had the strong desire to call my father to let him know I where I was headed, but then I remembered that there is a pretty good chance that nobody even knows Uncle Howard's phone number, or if he even has a phone.

I got into the beach town a little before noon after stopping for another gross lunch, and a few walks with Bahama. I ended up having to call my parents anyway because I couldn't remember his exact address, despite remembering the Christmas card he sent my parents fairly well, a bunch of Santa's sitting around a poker table smoking and drinking. Luckily my mother, who keeps almost everything, was able to locate the card and envelope within a couple minutes. Plus, if she hadn't found the card, I'm sure she had already put his address in her handy dandy address book. After talking to my folks for a few minutes, and telling them about my trip to that point, including worrying my mother with the wallet story, I hung up right outside my uncle's house.

The huge house sat on stilts to protect it from flooding due to hurricanes causing some kind of impact on this little town every few years. Four parking spots were underneath the house, and then a wooden staircase went all the way up to the third floor. As soon as I parked the car Bahama got excited – more than usual.

It was pretty dark underneath the house, but I could see well enough to know that we were being greeted by a huge dog. The mix breed dog appeared to come in at over 100 pounds. I felt Bahama and I had every right to be scared, but in demeanor the dog was calm, as it peaked into the driver's side window. After giving us a curious look, he backed up and sat at the foot of the steps. I guess he was going to be our personal escort on our way to meet Howard and his wife. Judging by the size of his back, he would have had no trouble taking my luggage for me.

Bahama and I got out of the car, Bahama making

a bee-line directly to the beast of a dog for an introduction. This scared me a bit, but the dog hardly paid any attention to Bahama, other than a quick sniff back, and then looked back at me, as if to ask, "Are you coming?" Being that I had spent most of the time talking to a dog the last two days, I didn't feel odd at all, answering, "We're coming! We're coming!"

We marched up to the third floor, and around to the side of the house facing the Gulf of Mexico. As soon as we reached the final step, we were greeted by a hot tub with my naked uncle and his second wife, whom I had not yet met mind you – not that it would have made it any easier had I met her. My uncle barely moved, while his wife Gail looked around frantically weighing her decisions about running into the house stark naked or sinking further into the hot tub. At this point to her I was just a stranger, so she also had the concern of just exactly who was this guy standing in front of her and staring at her. Unintentionally. I was also worried that she would scream or squeal and that their dog would react by eating me for lunch. Luckily, after a few seconds of remembrance, my uncle said to his wife, "Relax, relax, this is my brother's kid, Michael," setting down a now-soggy joint on an elevated table next to the hot tub.

I don't think this helped Gail any, as she was still naked, and I was still a stranger. I finally got the hint and walked a few steps back down the stairs. I was used to back tracking this trip so this was natural. I waited until I could tell she had scampered back into the house.

In the meantime, Howard had put on a pair of swimming trunks and was getting out of the tub.

"Your dad said you were driving around the country. I had a feeling you might make it here," slapping a wet hand on my back. "I see you met my wife," he added, laughing, as she came back outside, this time with clothes on, but still wearing a red mask of embarrassment.

While I had had the opportunity to get a full look at her I had diverted my eyes, until this point. She was a pretty woman, about my uncle's age, mid 40's. My first aunt, Howard's first wife, had been a bit overweight due to their eating habits, but Gail was a pillar of health. She had a flat stomach, toned arms and legs, and beautiful skin. Just as I was surmising that she was not the type of eater that my uncle is, or maybe was, she asked me while extending her arm for a handshake, "Are you hungry can I make you something?" making that the first time I had ever heard the possibility of homemade food an option in my uncle's presence.

"Yeah, hate to ask you do that being I just got here, but I am pretty hungry," as the gigantic sandwich I had eaten for breakfast was starting to wear off.

"Great, I'll make us some smoothies, and fresh salmon with wild rice. How's that sound?"

"Great, thank you," I said, as she was heading towards the kitchen in no-time.

Despite not seeing my uncle in quite a few years, I gave him a look as if to say, "What's up with this?"

"Yeah, I don't eat quite as bad as I used to." Seeing that my face had turned to a frown, concerned for his health, he quickly added, "Don't worry, I'm healthy, so it's nothing like that. Gail said if she was going to marry me and follow me around from here to there that I had to eat a bit healthier. To put it like she did, 'I'm not going to eat this shit for the rest of my life.' Loving her like I do, I agreed, but don't worry Mike, I still have my favorite places."

I whispered, "Does she know you still eat out?"

He replied, "Of course, we don't hold secrets from each other," but after a laugh he added, "I just usually don't tell her about it."

I sat down next to him in a beach chair, and for the next hour over lunch I told them what I had done so far. Gail was almost moved to tears when I told them about reconciling with my sister and niece. They also both got a chuckle when I told them about my wallet, and even offered to give me the money I had lost.

I asked them about their dog, who was off with Bahama giving her the lay of the land, sniffing through the sand in the front yard.

"Oh, that's Snuka. Funniest thing – one night, not long after we moved out here, he came up to us when we got back to the house after a walk, scaring the shit out of us." They both laughed.

They added, "But that's not the funny part. After we saw he was calm and nice and all that, we noticed he had on loin-cloths like the old wrestler Jimmy 'Superfly' Snuka!" More laughs followed, this time from me too.

"After calling the local shelter and leaving some signs up throughout the island nobody claimed him, so he became ours. For a beach dog he's terrified of the water, but as you can see, he loves the sand. He usually shakes most of it off before going into the house, but it feels like we are changing the sheets every day."

"Yeah, because you let him sleep in bed with us," Gail added, with a smile.

After some more light talking, my uncle asked, "So, what are you doing here?"

Taken slightly aback, but keeping up with the jovial feel of the conversation I just laughed, not knowing how to answer. "Good question."

"Ahh, I know that feeling all too well, I think you have some of my blood in you after all." Before I could say anything he added, "I've been where you are many times, maybe not with as heavy heart as you, but I have always felt like I am searching for something. While I figure out exactly what I'm looking for I figured I'd do it in the most beautiful places I could surround myself with. As you can see, we have plenty of beauty, and we have plenty of room, so you are welcome to stay as long as you want."

Gail nodded her approval of his invite. That's how Bahama and I ended up staying in Treasure Island for the next month.

9

It had been maybe ten years since I had been high – I mean really high. I had smoked a few times at cookouts, parties, and a concert or two, but I hardly ever felt any differently afterwards. With Howard and Gail around it was going to be hard not to be high. They celebrate almost every occasion with the words, "Let's get high." Going to the grocery store? Let's get high. We're going for a walk. Let's get high. I need to get air in the tires. Let's get high! I want to get high! Let's get high!

While not an authority on this topic, I was assured what I was smoking was "good shit." I felt that my uncle and aunt are nice enough people to get connections in every city that they live in, and that's how they always had a healthy supply of "herb," as they like to call it. However, when this came up one night my uncle told me they have been using the same supplier for close to 25 years. Perhaps, sometimes, it's different types of weed, but always the same supplier.

Their supplier, a couple with whom they had become good friends, lived in Arizona. Uncle Howard met Zeke and Callie when they were vacationing in Phoenix one winter. Howard said he knew he wouldn't last long in Phoenix because it wasn't close enough to a large enough body of water, but as a consolation prize, he did find a source to make sure his weed never ran out. I was told Zeke and Callie grew weed out of their basement, and have connections all over the world to other forms of herb.

Knowing Howard wasn't venturing to Phoenix every time he ran low, I asked him how he stayed stocked on one of my first days as his roommate.

He replied, "I know you're family, and I love you like the son I never had, but I'd rather not answer that."

I respected his response, and didn't press for an answer. I was free to use my imagination. Whatever I was smoking with him sure did help my imagination. I just figured a weed stork brought it to him during one of my hazy daydreams while staring out in the Gulf.

Even though there was no pressure from my uncle or aunt to do much of anything, I was again getting the desire to write. It's odd to think that smoking a ton of weed would make want me to do anything other than eat, but I think it was because of my chemical-filled brain I was getting antsy to get something out. It's no coincidence, I thought, especially while feeling like this, that it seemed most writers needed a little extra motivation, if you will, to be the best writer they can be. Inspiration has to come from somewhere, right?

A few peers in my college writing class and I would get a case of beer, and sit around one of our crappy apartments. Only a few beers in and I think everyone experienced a wave of inspiration. Occasionally, we would go from wanting to write books to wanting to write movies. The problem with combining drinking and writing is the fine line where you feel inspired and the point you start to get too drunk to even operate a pen. By the time our little group graduated we had at least a half dozen "scripts" started. My favorite one was the one we started on the inside of a pizza box. The main character was a pizza delivery driver. Imagine that.

So I don't know if it was the weed, or my surroundings, or that I just generally missed it, but I started seeking out part-time writing jobs again. For most of my marriage I made a living taking in all kinds of freelance jobs. When I was much younger I fancied myself a Hunter S. Thompson, always wanting to be part of the story, but there weren't many opportunities for me to do that. Instead I settled for becoming a semi-professional biography writer, usually writing a famous person's entire story in 1,000 words or less.

Through the years there have been many jobs. One of the big (see: financially rewarding) jobs I had was writing a biography on every president in the history of the United States, again in 1,000 words or less. The stories were to be given to an editor of an 8th grade history book, and then they would put the information I gave them in the context of the textbook. You had to be incredibly unbiased and neutral in your writing. It helped to have a grip on American history, but really anyone with a competent internet search function, and an 8th grade writing ability, could have done the job.

I also worked for various magazines, ranging from news, sports, and, even once, professional wrestling. For a while in college I had gotten into the habit of just applying for any job I could, trying to earn enough money to buy an engagement ring. A wrestling magazine, much to my surprise, asked me if I would rank the order of WrestleMania events from worst to first. I had been a bit of a wrestling fan in my youth, but at the time of the writing and since then, I hadn't watched wrestling in years. So, I watched every WrestleMania and sought out the opinions of people who I knew that watched wrestling. It was interesting watching over 60 hours of wrestling, but at the end I felt like I had a pretty good grip on it. For the record, I picked WrestleMania V as the best. The backlash was strong.

As the years passed during my college and young

adult years, my desire to write a novel grew stronger. Snapping back to a haze of reality on my uncle's deck, I decided that's what I would do then, only I would use a computer and not a pizza box. I had tried many times before to write a novel, but usually after a few thousand words I would think it was awful, and quit. Then after a few more months I would try again, then rinse and repeat. Another false start.

In the year of my mourning, I began to get the strong urge to write again, especially the last few weeks when I decided I was going to hit the road for an adventure of my own. From time to time I wrote short stories of imaginary adventures and a character similar to me took shape. I didn't think they were that good, but I shared some with my friends and family, and they seemed to be well received, but then again they didn't want to hurt the already fragile feelings of someone they cared about.

Most asked me if I had done the things the characters had done in the story, and almost always the answer was no. I know it wasn't their intention to make me feel upset with that question, but it always reminded me that for the last year, and in a lot of ways long before that, I hadn't done much of anything that would be considered an adventure. Those innocent questions ultimately helped lead me on this journey.

My wife always made more money than me. When she died I was left with what we had already had, plus a very substantial check from the insurance company. We always agreed with each other that if one of us were to die, we'd want the other to live relatively worry free. My wife and I didn't live exactly frugally, but we never bought things we didn't need, we didn't eat out much, preferring dinner with my family, who loved to cook, and we saved quite a bit. I was lucky enough to have a wife who supported my passion for writing. In freelance work, there could be long lulls between employment and then there was the amount of time I'd have to spend building up a resume so I could realistically have a chance at the big jobs, which were few and far between.

Early on in our relationship I took jobs that paid one and two cents per word. I also did all the filler jobs as I called them. Basically, I just provided content page after content page for new websites so they seem established when they first hit the web. This was mind-numbing work, but it eventually began to pay off with stories in magazines and newspapers. Still, without my wife supporting me, there is no way I would have been able to have the time to build a decent resume. It was a catch-22. I had to do all of the work, which equaled hours and hours of time, but little pay, just hoping for the pot of gold at the end of the crap rainbow. There's no way I could have put the time in doing that on my own. I would have had to support myself in another way, or I would have starved. Or just ate a lot more meals that my mommy cooked.

Still, after six or seven years of writing, if you can call it that, I wasn't sure if I was doing it for the love of writing, or the love of money. I can remember many occasions when I had the idea to sit down and write something for myself – a short story, a novel, a screenplay idea, and I would think to myself, I'm not getting paid for this, why am I writing this? It's just the way my brain had become, and maybe still is, wired. When one gets used to getting paid for something for so long it's hard to do it "just for fun." I often wondered if athletes, musicians, and even healthcare professionals have similar thoughts. Time after time I would get something going, but never had the desire to do go through with it.

It was a conversation with my dad that helped changed my view on my struggling with writing. My dad and I weren't much for deep conversation, but the handful of times I really sought his advice he always came through. He doesn't waste words, and thinks carefully before he talks. Many people say multiple things in hopes of hitting the target. When my dad spoke, he almost always hits the bull's eye on the first shot.

It was about ten months after she died, and he and I were talking on my deck. He heard my whole speech about how I was having a hard time finding the desire to do writing I wasn't being paid for.

"You'll write when you want to. When something moves you enough to write, you will," he said.

"Also son, all that money stuff you say doesn't make sense, at least to me."

"Why"?

"Because, if you were to write a movie, or a script, or a novel, or whatever, and it were to sell, you would be making a whole lot more money than you've ever made writing about dead presidents. Hell, you'd have all the dead presidents you'd ever need," laughing at his own joke that I suspect he didn't intend to make until it came out. But he was right.

I guess I ultimately knew that if I were to ever sell something it would most likely be for a decent chance of money, but it wasn't that part of what he had said that I focused on. I'd write when I was ready, he had said to me. There was no need to force anything, in other words. I have thought about his words often since that day – all the way up to the dead presidents joke - and they have steered me straight when I began to have anxiety about what I was, and what I wasn't, accomplishing in the writing world. There, on the deck of my Uncle Howard's beach house, was when I decided it was time to start writing again. Without major money concerns, and no real concerns beyond finding a bed to sleep in at the end of the night, I was ready to write for myself.

10

For the next few weeks I walked around town with Bahama and sometimes Snuka, although Snuka was so big he tended to scare fellow pedestrians. I snuck off for meals with my uncle that my aunt would never have approved of, smoked a lot, and wrote.

After more than a year of not writing I didn't really know where to start. I have a writer friend who always told me, "When in doubt, just write…" I usually just try to remember that part of the quote, but inevitably he always ends with "…something that's not complete crap should eventually come out."

I wrote about my wife, I wrote about my sister, I wrote about the GA Pig Shack, I wrote about my dog, and I wrote about myself. After writing for about a week, while sitting on the deck, I noticed something funny about my writing, something that I must have trained myself to do. I write in 1,000 word chunks because that's how many words I used to write on my presidential biographies. It didn't matter what I was writing about, I would get to 1,000 words or so, and just run out of things to say. Also because 1,000 words generally signified the end of a workday for me, I usually found it hard to continue writing after I met my quota, especially those first few weeks.

Day after day, not just at my uncle's, but for the entire duration of the trip, I had to reprogram my brain, and write just for the act of writing. This should be simple, but when all you have to do is write, it can be pretty intimidating. It wasn't that the environment I was in wasn't an excellent one for writing. I had a giant beach house, with decks protruding from all sides, so I had multiple places to re-hone my craft. My uncle and aunt were always close by if I wanted to talk, but never intrusive, and looking back on it, I don't think they ever asked what I was writing about. They were just genuinely happy I was writing again. Aunt Gail was always quick to have a meal for us, but just like my uncle would tell me in secret, her meals were usually too grainy, green, and cardboard-ish for my taste. I usually had an appetite because of the other green I was partaking in, which I could also thank my uncle and aunt for, so it all worked out.

That month I also spent a lot of time at the beach. When I was young, Howard had taught me how to boogie board when my parents used to visit him in whatever beach town he was living in that particular summer. I tried boogie boarding again, but after a few looks from the local kids who actually knew what they were doing, I reverted back to just walking on the shoreline mostly, which was fine.

Sometimes I would bring the dogs down to the beach. Bahama loved the water, usually scaring me because I always thought she was going too deep, but she always came back onto the beach wearing a grin to cancel out my fears. Now Snuka, as Gail had mentioned, was another story. Snuka loved the sand, but absolutely hated getting too close to the ocean. There was an imaginary force field that only Snuka could see maybe 15 feet from the ocean. When he crossed it, it would send him into doggy panic attacks. A few times Bahama and I would go a few feet into the ocean to play around. Snuka, wanting no part of it, would bark at us the entire time, showing his displeasure. It was even worse when Howard and Gail would join us. It was almost as if Snuka refused to believe his masters could defy him by going into the ocean. Snuka wouldn't bark when they went in.

Instead, he would turn his back completely to the ocean, and dig a hole. This was no small hole, being able to fit a large dog, and Snuka would lay in it until Gail and Howard came out of the ocean, safely back on the right side of the force field. Just like that he would snap out of it and be a happy dog again. Some beach dog.

A few days before I decided I would be leaving the friendly confines of Howard, Gail, and Treasure Island, I was feeling like it was time to go. I most likely imagined it, but I felt like I was wearing out my welcome. I think I was just eager to get on with the next part of my journey. One night, walking back from an organic restaurant in town Gail insisted we visit, the topic of my next location came up.

"What's next?" asked Howard, as I saw him eyeballing the ice cream shop we would have surely went in had we not been with Gail.

"Hmmm, I really don't know." I really didn't know.

It was during this walk on Main Street that I realized that for the first time in my journey I was going to most likely end up someplace I didn't know anybody. This caused me some anxiety, but it was that being on my own feeling I was craving that originally inspired me to go on this trip.

"How about the Florida Keys? Hemingway lived there; isn't he your favorite author?" He continued with a laugh, "If it was good enough for him, it's surely good enough for you."

"I agree." I said, and I did.

11

The drive to the beginning of the Florida Keys took about six hours, but because I was heading to the southernmost point in the United States, Key West, it took another two hours. What I mean to say is that it would have taken another two hours if I would have driven straight there. Instead we made a stop along the way, adding another hour to our trip.

The beginning of the Keys is sort of like driving into a new state, but that analogy doesn't really do it justice. For example, when you are driving into Georgia from South Carolina, you don't see any discernible differences except a sign welcoming you to the birth place of Jimmy Carter. Entering the Keys is almost like driving into an entirely different place unlike anywhere else in America.

What you first notice is that there is a two-lane highway on both sides of the road separated by a median. If you are heading south, you are driving along the Gulf of Mexico. If you are heading north, you are driving along the Atlantic Ocean. These two sides of the road are simply known as the "bay side" or the "ocean side" by the locals. To get to nearly any place on this stretch of road I learned you need to only have two questions answered. Question #1: What mile marker? Question #2: Which side? There are neighborhoods as you travel, but 99 percent of the restaurants and tourists attractions on the way to Key West can be found by following those two simple directions.

Shortly after getting into Key Largo, the first main Key, and perhaps the most popular one thanks largely, in part, to the Beach Boys song "Kokomo,"

Bahama made a sound that indicated she had to use the bathroom, and quick. I pulled into a hotel resort called Kona Kai. At first I was just going to let Bahama do her duty and head right back into the car, but the palm trees, and the view of the Gulf through those trees appearing to me from the parking lot, had us off and walking.

I saw the building that was both the lobby and office. I didn't think much of it because I had no intention of staying at this place seeing that I wasn't planning on spending as much money as I thought this place would cost nightly, but as I got closer I noticed works of art in the building. Not much of an art appreciator, I was surprised when I found myself walking through the door. Looking back on it, I believe I walked in because of the promise of air conditioning. While the temperature wasn't extraordinarily hot, I was already sweating buckets because of the humidity, which ranks up there as the highest percentage in America, on average. Walking in, a woman sitting behind a desk with her bare feet visible under a typical office desk, introduced herself to me and Bahama, and we responded by returning introductions to Becky.

Becky, it turned out, is the primary owner of the property, sharing the duties with two other partners. She said she enjoys the day-to-day of running the smallish, yet beautiful property, and asked me if I liked art.

"Ummm, yeah" I said, glowing red. I wasn't a big fan of art, but I was a big fan of talking to Becky.

I suspected Becky figured out that I didn't have a clue about art, but she was nice enough to continue anyway. "Well, here we have a large display of statues, mostly created by local artists, and some of the best photographs, all original, of many of the popular places in the Keys."

It was near the end of her description of her property that I casually looked at a four foot work of art, an intertwined body's statue, symbolizing God knows what. I then examined the price tag – $50,000. The shock of the price physically caused me to jerk, and take a step backwards, right into another four foot statue, which I heard rocking on its pedestal. I was temporarily paralyzed with dread, unable to turn around for fear I would certainly knock it over.

Somehow I made a move where I stayed facing the $50,000 statue, but reached my hands behind my back. Luckily, I was able to grab on to the tusk of the four foot elephant, preventing it from causing the most expensive domino effect in history. When order was restored, I checked out the price tag on the tusk – $75,000.

"All prices are negotiable," she said, before adding with a laugh, "unless you break them all first."

As I was ready to make a beeline to the door, and to the safe haven of my car, she spoke.

"The sun's getting ready to set, would you like to go to the dock and watch it with me"? Her voice didn't suggest she was making a move on her clumsy customer, instead just asking a question she would have asked to any man, woman, child, or dog who happened to be standing with her at that moment.

Weighing my options, I thought of two scenarios: I'd find some way to fall into the water, or something equally embarrassing. I was just figuring out that my safest option would be getting into my car and continue driving when Becky spoke. "Come on, it's a Keys tradition!" Bahama accepted the invite, so I had no choice but to follow. After all, at that point in my life there weren't too many attractive women, or any women for that matter, inviting me to do anything lately.

Becky walked towards the deck, and I was surprised to see so many people, maybe around 30, taking up various spots to watch the sunset. This didn't seem to surprise Becky at all, as she explained that not only did the property have 14 rooms, but many people driving by at this time often stop to watch the sunset.

It's hard to explain a sunset and what makes one particularly better in one place more so than the other. The sun, after all, is the same for everyone even a million miles away, but by just changing your view of the setting sun, you see something you have taken for granted all your life.

The climax of the sun setting lasts about 20 minutes, with varying degrees of sun beams bouncing off the water in every angle possible. The last few minutes are the most exciting, watching the sun close up shop for the night by going behind the curtain that is the horizon known as the Gulf. This evening, unfortunately for some, due to the placement of the sun, they didn't get a clear view. I personally didn't mind this, but this was the first time I had ever heard anyone let out disapproving sighs, just short of boos, when it came to a setting sun.

Seconds after the sun had gone to bed, Becky reinforced the idea that she wasn't interested in me. "Thanks for stopping by. Is there anything else I can do for you?"

As I was stammering through another answer, Bahama made a beeline towards the end of the pier, dodging the legs of tourists and locals in the process. Before I could say a thing or even gasp, she leapt into the water. I knew Bahama could swim, but I didn't hesitate, running towards the point of the pier where she had jumped in. I briefly remember that during my dart towards Bahama that Becky was watching me run, another one of my awkward moments.

Becky ran behind, and was able to make sense of what was happening before I could. While I was running, if you can call it that, I heard Becky say that the Gulf was only a few feet all around, meaning I could jump in if I had to with no real fear. That information helped calm me down as I reached the end of the pier. As I looked down I saw two creatures, not including Bahama, near a bubbling manmade spring. I have no idea how Bahama knew they were there, or if she did before she decided to jump in. My heart stopped beating as fast when I noticed Bahama was neither trying to attack the creatures, or being attacked by them, instead just swimming with them.

"Those are manatees; we've sort of adopted them as mascots. They come up to the pier around this time about once a week. I guess your dog just wanted to introduce herself." I later learned that these fountains are a bit of a controversial subject in the Keys. Many people, particularly longtime residents of the Keys, don't think that natural things should be at all manipulated by manmade objects, such as this fountain. Fresh water fountains attract manatees.

Of course, now I was embarrassed again. Between nearly breaking thousands of dollars of art and now Bahama jumping into the water, perhaps scaring away the "mascots" from ever returning again, it had been quite the last half an hour. Thankfully the manatees seemed hardly interested at all in Bahama. I guess when you have people reaching into the water to touch you day after day and swimming with all the other animals in the gulf, a little dog isn't going to be much of a bother. Still I felt my damage was done.

After Bahama had her fun, she swam back to the

shore, and shook herself dry and returned to my side as if nothing had happened. Becky, who had laughed during the entire ordeal, told me repeatedly not to worry about it. "If anything, you gave all these people a good show," many were still staring at Bahama and me.

Before I came close to destroying anything else, man-made or living, I thanked Becky for her hospitality, and made a brisk walk for my car. For good measure, Bahama took a long pee on a lizard statue right next to the parking lot. I didn't dare turn around to see if Becky was still watching.

12

I called a bed and breakfast in Key West, Frank and Jean's, where I made plans to stay. In my mind, choosing a bed and breakfast, as opposed to a traditional hotel, had a more romantic quality about it. Fortunately for me, Key West is pretty animal-friendly, at least for the independently owned places, so I had a few choices to pick from. But, Frank and Jean's won out in the end. Lucky them.

I always choose a place that has free breakfast in the morning, or at least built into the price. Also, the pictures online featuring a beautiful pool in their backyard helped seal the deal, though I hardly used it my entire time there. It only has six rooms, but it was just a couple of blocks from Duval Street, the center of the action, meaning if things got too wild, it was a short walk back to my room.

When I parked, I was stunned to see how big the place was. I later learned it used to be the mansion of a successful businessman during Key West's infancy. I was greeted almost immediately by a motherly-looking woman who introduced herself as Jean, who walked me into the "front room" which acted as registration when guests arrived, and a place for people to hang out when they just want to get away from the heat and humidity for a few minutes. During the day there was always a tray of ice cold water sitting on a table just inside the front door. I don't think this was done for the tourists, because they would have had no way of knowing they were welcome inside. It was instead for the local working population that had to walk to and from their jobs, often in the sweltering weather. Nice touch.

After telling me a little about the property, Jean checked me in and insisted on taking my bags, showing me to my room. The room wasn't as big as I thought it would be from the outside, but it was just fine. It had a full size bed, a small desk with a lamp on a table on one side of the bed, and a small older-style TV in the right corner. In front of the bed was a storage chest. In the other corner were two doors, behind one was a small kitchen, complete with stove, and the other was a bathroom.

Jean opened the two windows in the room before I could protest, but realized she was probably doing this to get some of the muggy air out of the room. She also blasted a wall unit A/C. It was loud, but effective. Jean explained that she could have the room cleaned every day, even if I just left for 20 minutes. I thought of asking her how she would know if I was there or not, but with six rooms, I guessed she knew who was there and who was not. Breakfast is served at 8 a.m. daily, dinner at 5 p.m., and there was a refrigerator that had bottled water and fresh fruit, which I was free to help myself to at anytime. It was only about 8:00 p.m., but after the long drive, my art store antics, and Bahama's swim, I was pretty beat. Before too long I crashed onto the bed.

The next sound I heard sounded like a child screaming, and a loud crashing. Between not remembering where I was, and being unable to locate a light, I was soon in a panic. After a few seconds of being awake, my senses came back to me guided by the light peeking in from the open window. There was a cat in the room, and Bahama was obsessed with getting to it. Bahama generally likes cats, but with me asleep and being in a new area, she had turned into my little guard dog.

I figured out by doing my best Sherlock

impersonation that the cat must have entered through the open window. I was just telling Bahama to settle down when I spotted the digital clock on the desk, it was easier to find now that the lamp had crashed to the floor thanks to our early morning intruder. 2:16 a.m. Knock – Knock – Knock.

"Everything okay in there?" asked a man from the other side of the door.

"A cat's in here going crazy – got in through the window," I replied, trying to direct the cat to one of the two open windows and protecting myself from the cat's claws. I was hoping Bahama didn't follow the cat out the window.

He must not have heard me over the hissing. I heard a key turn, and he came in. Rather calmly he asked me to put my dog into the kitchen and picked up the cat and placed it outside of the window.

"Hey, I'm Frank, Jean's husband. I guess she didn't tell you," he said, while reaching out and shaking my hand. "We started leaving food out for the cats down in the courtyard by the pool, and they sort of became part of the charm of the place. A lot of people come here just because of the cats. They've grown accustomed to coming into visitors' rooms."

First, I apologized profusely for waking him up, and everyone else within a three mile radius, but he just said, "Don't worry about it; it happens all the time. Jean usually forgets to tell our guests about the cats, and sometimes I don't get to you all in time. If you don't want them to come in, just shut the windows. They have their regular shots, so there's nothing to worry about, unless you're paying for them," he added with a tired chuckle.

I liked the idea of cats coming in out of the heat, and even though I wouldn't mind leaving out food and water myself I knew I would have to make sure

Bahama was okay with the idea before trying that. My parents had cats, so she was used to them, so I figured it wouldn't be a problem once Bahama got used to the way things worked around there.

Frank once again told me to not worry about the disruption and to enjoy my stay, but after that start I knew I wasn't going to sleep anymore. My stomach was growling, having not eaten much that day, so I went quietly downstairs to the refrigerator that I was told held the fresh fruit. I guess most of the supply of fruit had yet to been restocked, so all I saw was water and a type of fruit I had never seen before. My stomach was growling in anticipation of food, so I gave the mystery fruit a go.

The fruit was a yellowish green color, which I could see from the glow of a street light through a window in the downstairs kitchen because I hadn't turned on the light. It was very oddly shaped, with what felt like ruffles. I didn't know where to start. I just sunk my teeth into it, and once I got through the sour outside I was met with a delicious sweet flavor in the middle. A couple minutes into making a mess of my face and shirt due to the dripping sticky juice, a light turned on. The embarrassments never end, I thought.

"Most people cut that first," declared Jean, before heading into the kitchen and grabbing a knife and plate. She saw me rubbing my face with the back of my hand, so she also handed me a paper towel. Jean then grabbed another one of the fruits from the fridge, cut it up into clean slices, and held up one when she finished. "Star fruit. Can you guess how they got their name?"

I couldn't remember the last time I needed someone to cut my food for me, but was thankful Jean was there. Over three or four more star fruits, this time with me cutting them, I told her about what I was doing on this trip. I spoke about my wife, but didn't get into too many details.

Jean didn't speak much but I could tell she was listening, and it was very therapeutic for me. She reminded me of my mother in a lot of ways, but was quieter. She was the type of person, the kind I had met just a few times in my life, where she almost commanded me to spill my soul without saying a signal word. She didn't offer much in the way of advice, but instead just listened.

It was nearly 3 a.m. when our conversation wrapped-up. I could tell she was getting even more tired because she was speaking less and less, but over the weeks I learned Frank did most of the talking in their union, which seemed just fine for Jean.

Before heading to bed, Jean told me of a few restaurants within walking distance that stayed open 24 hours, so if I found myself hungry at that hour during my stay to check those out. I also suspected she told me this so I didn't wake her up at odd hours of the night. I was a bit of an oaf when it came to getting around a kitchen.

Heading out of the kitchen, leaving me at the table, she told me I was free to stay as long as I want, and she wouldn't make plans to rent out my room until I told her I was leaving. She also mentioned that I could pay a weekly rate, which would save me about 100 bucks a week, as opposed to paying daily, if I thought I was staying for an extended period of time. She knew I was planning to stay for an extended amount of time before I did.

During the drive from Treasure Island, I had dreaded thinking about how I was actually going to be on my own for possibly the first time in my life. As I sat there alone in the kitchen, I thought about how I wasn't nearly as on my own as I expected. Jean, as mentioned, reminded me of my mom, and after listening and showing a genuine interest in my life, I felt safe around her. I knew I would be comfortable with Jean and Frank looking after me, or at least having the feeling they would.

With a full belly, I went back to my room and slept soundly for a few more hours. Waking up around 6 a.m., I hung out in my room for a couple hours, showering and writing, and headed downstairs for breakfast. I wasn't expecting much more than a continental breakfast, but was instead greeted by a meal fit for a farmer. Ham, sausage, bacon, eggs, potatoes, biscuits, and freshly squeezed Florida orange juice, and of course, star fruit.

I usually wasn't a big breakfast eater, but just like my mom, Jean was the type of person who would make sure you've eaten at least one full plate before she thought you were properly stocked to start your day. Being that this was a Wednesday, and not at full capacity, I knew that this was going to be the size of breakfast every day, at least. I resigned myself to the fact that this portion of the trip was not going to be a stop where I would be eating healthy.

Following breakfast, I went back upstairs for a few more hours to do some writing. I had intended to write for even longer, but being in Key West this long without seeing the sights was getting to me, and most likely hurting my writing if all I was thinking about was getting out of my room.

After setting Bahama up in the room, knowing she does well alone for a few hours on her own, and of course closing the windows, I headed out. I would have normally taken Bahama on a walk like this, but because I wasn't sure where I was going I thought it was best to leave her behind until I had a bit of an idea of my surroundings.

It was a short walk from my room to the epicenter of Key West, Duval Street. It houses most of the restaurants and bars tourists like to frequent. During the short walk to Duval Street I thought about how my uncle had told me Hemingway had lived here and how he walked these same exact streets some 70 years earlier. From what I understood, from reading biographies and some internet research, he spent most of his time walking between his house which is now a museum and known as the Hemingway House, and the bar Sloppy Joe's. Occasionally, legend states, he took his work to the bar and did it there. In my modern day thought it was hard for me not to imagine him lugging his laptop with him to the bar, which would have been quite the sight. However, he was bringing paper and pen, which makes for an even better sight. I couldn't help but wonder if he ever spilled any of his drinks on his writings. I pictured his legendary temper getting the better of him, tossing the glass to the side while frantically running into the street, hoping the sun would dry his page before he lost a passage he may not be able to remember depending on how much he drank.

I knew that many drinks are associated with Hemingway, mainly because he enjoyed many drinks. While in Cuba he preferred a mojito, but 90 miles away in Key West, he enjoyed a daiquiri or martini. He has also been associated with the on and off again legalized absinthe. It's funny, Hemingway is arguably known more for his renowned drinking than his writing, so it's no big surprise that a debate on exactly which drinks he drank and when he drank them is easy to come across, specifically online. I know drinking stories can be legendary, but I can't imagine a more legendary drinker than Hemingway.

Despite being around noon, I could see by my fellow passersby that this was plenty late to start drinking. I wasn't, nor am I now, a big drinker, but being that I think Hemingway had a large part of me finding my way down here, I thought I'd have a "when in Key West" experience. Why not follow in the footsteps of the most popular resident ever? I wasn't planning on discriminating on which Hemingway drinks I would ingest, thinking that the fairest way to get the most out of my experience. I mentally retraced my steps back to the house, because in a few hours I figured those steps would be hazy.

A short walk up Duval I found Sloppy Joe's, and I entered as the morning turned to afternoon. I'm guessing I wasn't the first want-to-be writer attempting to follow in Hemingway's footsteps the employees had ever seen come through their doors, but I was very excited to be in a place of history.

After bellying up to the bar, I ordered a daiquiri, which prompted the young male bartender to ask, "Do you want a straight or a Hemingway daiquiri?"

"Hemingway daiquiri? I didn't know there was such a thing." Thinking it was just a tourist-trap type drink, probably a few more dollars than a regular.

The bartender sat a glass and towel down and assumed the position of someone who was about to give a lecture. "You see, Hemingway was a diabetic."

"He was? I had no idea."

"Yes," he answered quickly, returning to his lecture. "He would sometimes order a regular daiquiri, but most of the time he replaced the sugar with grapefruit juice. He'd also add a hint of maraschino liquor – the actual liquor, not just the juice that comes with the cherries.

"Oh, well thanks for educating me, I'll take a

Hemingway then," I said.

"Great," he said, pleased that he got to educate a tourist today.

As he walked away, a gentleman to my left with a deep tan, wearing a Panama Jack hat, buttoned-up flowery shirt, khakis, flip flops, and a beer in front of him – a local I presumed – began talking to me.

"If he was really interested in educating you, he'd tell you that Hemingway never actually stepped foot in this bar."

"What?" I laughed uncomfortably, thinking this was a joke or a riddle of some kind going over my head.

"Sure, he drank quite a bit of the drink you just ordered, but he did it around the corner there on Greene."

Over the course of my first daiquiri, and second, the man wearing the khaki shorts who never revealed his name, not that I would have remembered anyway, gave me a history lesson about two popular bars in Key West.

For a large portion of the 1930's, the bar known as Sloppy Joe's was in an establishment around the corner, the actual drinking hole of Hemingway. In 1938, the owner of Sloppy Joe's saw the rent of the building that housed his bar raise considerably. As the tale goes, the landlord seemed to think that because the bar was so popular the owners would have no problems paying the increased rent. The landlord was correct in just half that statement – it was no problem – for the whole bar to shut down and move around the corner onto Duval Street where they received lower rent, and continued as if nothing happened. Thing is, Hemingway was already out of town by the time Sloppy Joe's took up its new residence, having left town just a couple of years prior.

"In other words, if you want to really drink where Hemingway drank you'll have to move your solo party around the corner to Captain Tony's," said my own personal professor.

While the daiquiris were good, and my bar stool had seemed to rise by three feet, I bid the man adieu and headed around the corner.

Being that Key West is known for Duval Street, and not Greene Street, this road, and this establishment, were far less crowded than the one I had just come from. Now, this is how I pictured Hemingway's Key West. In a place like the current Sloppy Joe's, especially if it were modern day, Hemingway would have been pestered by autograph and picture seekers between every drink of his daiquiri. It's hard to imagine that he wouldn't have said, "The hell with this," and moved his drinking to his own sizable house – or at a place like Captain Tony's.

Despite seeming like less of a tourist trap than Joe's, Tony's still had a reminder here and there that Hemingway once walked those floors. The biggest reminder of that was a bar stool – THE barstool – that Hemingway sat on when he drank here. In addition to a bar stool with his name on it, there were ones with the names of Truman Capote, Shel Silverstein, John F. Kennedy, and Jimmy Buffett, among others. I chose the Walter Cronkite stool, as the Hemingway stool was taken just before I could scoop it up.

Here I ordered another daiquiri or three, and walked around. Despite losing the name "Sloppy Joe's" and most of Hemingway's tourist traffic to the establishment on Duval Street, this place holds tons more charm. I'll go out on a limb, perhaps the limb of the tree that sits right in the middle of Captain

Tony's, that if Hemingway came back today and had to choose between the two bars he'd most likely be sitting right next to me on his stool.

I learned from the bartender here, an older man named Hess, that the barstool with Buffett's name on it is usually warm, because whenever he is in Key West – his permanent residence – he does most of his drinking at Tony's. In fact, legend has it, he even wrote a song about this bar and its longtime owner, the captain himself, Tony Tarracino. Buffet will always be grateful to Tarracino because Buffet got his start there. The rumor is Tarracino usually paid him in tequila instead of cash. If you've heard just a few Buffet songs you get the impression that this arrangement was just fine with him.

Hess told me that Tarracino sold the bar in 1989, but still showed up once a week until his death in 2008 just to greet new customers and shoot the breeze with the long-standing ones. The new owner, of course, didn't mind Tarracino's presence because it brought in quite a revenue stream.

In addition to having a tree centered right in the middle of the bar, there are also thousands of business cards lining the walls, some of them 30 and 40 years old. It was almost enough for me to wish I had a business card of my own to post on the wall just to join the others.

Instead I figured I'd have to just sit down and drink with the others. After another, I began thinking of other Hemingway staples I could try. The Hemingway daiquiris were getting a little too sweet, and I was ready to try something else while I still could. Plus, I was getting the feeling that this wasn't a daiquiri type of place, unless you were ordering one for your female companion, one of which I didn't have by my side.

I automatically went to the most extreme thing I could think of. I wasn't even sure if what I wanted to order was legal, but because most of my inhibitions were out the door and somewhere on Greene Street, I placed my order.

"Hey Hess, are you able to make me an abs-absith...ummm absinthe."

Hess laughed "You're walking home, right"?

"Ahh, yeah just right around the corner," while awkwardly pointing in a direction that was most likely nowhere near Frank and Jean's place.

"Okay good enough. Well the absinthe we give you here isn't quite the same as what Hemingway drank. We have a watered-down version, if you will, but in your state I'm not sure it's going to make that much of a difference. And with nothing to compare it to, you won't know the difference anyway" he said with a straight face.

Based on the little I knew about the history of the drink, I was hoping for him to lay out an arrangement of silver spoons, or at the very least a cool-looking, hour-glass-shaped glass. Unfortunately, all Hess had for me was a basic high ball glass. First he filled it with a green color liquid that came out of a liquor bottle like any other. Once that was in the glass he took out a champagne bottle adding just a splash before sliding it over to me.

"A Hemingway absinthe, sir."

I thought about arguing about my lack of silver spoons, sugar cubes, and interesting looking glass, but thankfully I had enough of myself left to refrain. If this is what Hemingway drank, it was good enough for me.

It was the strongest taste I had ever experienced. I imagined I looked like I had just taken a bite out of a lemon, only a thousand times worse. Hess laughed at me, adding, "I wish I had a camera! You better drink all of that before the ghost of Hemingway comes after you."

There it was. The hook, line, and sinker for a drunk guy: a ghost story.

He judged my expression of confusion, saying "What? You didn't think Hemingway would grace that other establishment, did you?"

I had seen the Elvira Tombstone in the other room with the pool table, but took it as a joke. That, Hess told me is not a joke, and with the unique history of the old yellow building I was doing my drinking in, it would be more of a surprise if there weren't any ghosts. Turns out Hemingway's ghost is just one ghost that people have said they saw or heard while working or drinking here late at night.

Hess explained to me that the very building we were in was built in 1850, making it one of the oldest buildings in the city. The first business this building held was enough to make almost anyone believe in ghost stories – a morgue. In addition to being a morgue it was also the city's main supply of ice. I inquired to Hess about how many ice and morgue combinations still operate in the country. Hess, who laughed, chalked my question up to being drunk.

In the 1890's they shipped out the bodies and ice, and replaced it with some newfangled technology called a wireless telegraph station. The station became not only an important part of the history of Key West, but also the history of America. When the battleship Maine was sunk in April 1898, provoking the Spanish-American War, it was through this building that the rest of America heard the news. The sinking of Maine has been determined to be an accident when guns on board detonated, and not an actual act of war.

A decade later, the building became a cigar factory, housing thousands of Cuban cigars – back then they were easy to get; now, not so much. After a short stint as a cigar factory, it became a very popular place for the young men in the Navy who were traveling around the world – a bar that moonlighted as a bordello.

During prohibition, the building hardly missed a step, becoming the most popular speak-easy in the area. Hess said it hardly ever met any legal issues from local law enforcement – because, he added with an easy chuckle, "they were some of the biggest customers."

"That brings us to just about Hemingway's day. He lived in Key West on and off for about a decade, but around the time he left for the last time the owners took advantage of a cheaper rent around the corner, and moved there. This place went through a few names as a bar and finally was sold to Tony, and here we are."

Being as drunk as I was, it took a few trips to the bar before I finally got down the whole history. For my first visit, and a few after that, I couldn't get past the ghost stories. Luckily Hess was a patient man.

Hess told me that this was a popular place on the Key West ghost tour, and that of all the other places on the tour, this was the one that held the most allure because more people believe they felt the presence of another being here more than anywhere else.

Because of mixing drinking with ghost stories, I found myself thinking about my wife more than I had since I started the trip. I instantly hit a point of sorrow so strong that I was aware of Hess still talking, but she was all I could think of. While sitting on the Cronkite stool, I remembered when she died I would find myself pleading almost every night that she would give me a sign that everything would be okay, perhaps even in the form of a ghost. I just wanted to see any sign at all that what had happened made sense in any way at all.

Hess obviously didn't mean to offend me. In fact, at this point in our relationship he had no idea that I had ever been married, let alone a widower. Hess continued to try to make some more light talk that day, but after a while I told Hess I had to leave. He had no reason to ask me if something was wrong having just met me, but he did anyway. Later I would be thankful he cared about a stranger's sudden change of attitude, but that day I just said I had to go get my dog.

With a day that had started so excitingly, I was surprised even in my drunken state how quickly it had turned. Luckily, by the time I got back to Frank and Jean's house, the alcohol had made me very sleepy so I got some relief from myself when I passed out almost as soon as I walked back in the room. Jean must have taken Bahama out because she didn't act like she had to go when I got back to the room, but she always seemed to know when I was thinking about my wife and usually gave me distance. I fell asleep thinking about my wife and my dreams were filled with nightmares of her in her wedding dress walking around Captain Tony's, always just out of my reach.

13

I remember my first love. Puppy love. Teenage love. It was my freshman year of high school, and I was so enamored with the idea that a girl could like me. Because it was the first time a girl had admittedly liked me, it came along with a large amount of jealousy I still am not proud about to this day. A perfect mix of that jealousy, hormones, and typical teenage angst was a perfect cocktail for a lot of regrettable thoughts and actions.

Abby and I had been friends since elementary school, then things got awkward with us in middle school, as boy-girl relationships often do. In high school it seemed all the cool kids were dating, so Abby and I resorted back to our old elementary school days, only we were older and kissing each other more. I remember the emotions I had hijacked nearly every other thought I had. Concentrating on sports was out of the question most of the time because I was in my own world thinking about Abby and the thought of losing her to another guy almost constantly. Despite having a girlfriend, my self-esteem was weak.

Our boyfriend-girlfriend relationship lasted from the first week of junior year in high school until just before the end of the school year. In that time I think we broke up with each other at least a dozen times, mostly for just a day at a time. The drama consumed so much of me that it was routine for a basketball being passed to hit me square in the face or a baseball to land just a few feet away from me in the outfield, landing me seat on the bench next to a very angry coach.

Eventually, and rightfully so, my dear Abby tired of my jealous ways. I can remember being so ridiculous that I would ask to use the bathroom in class so I could walk by her class just to see if I could see her chatting with another guy. Plus, considering she was a cheerleader, and our cheerleading team was co-ed, I had to watch from the court – or more often the bench – as another guy perched her high up into the air, hand on her ass. In my mind, I always saw the guy go from staring at her ass and then at me with a smirk on his face.

After a while, being accused of doing things she wasn't doing eventually wore her out. I remember her breaking up with me. While I was upset, I figured she would call in a day or two, and we'd be "Mike and Abby" again. School ended. She went on vacation in Minnesota to see her family; she never called. When she got back a few weeks later she dropped off some of the things I had given her for her birthday and holidays – a mix CD, photos, my basketball jersey – and then I knew it was over. What was torture is that she lived right on the main road – the main road that was impossible to bypass if you wanted to go anywhere, meaning I passed her house almost every day. I still have vivid memories of me staring out the window at her house as we drove by in the family car. It's usually raining during these remembrances.

When school started back up I was shocked and hurt by how, in Abby's eyes, it looked like I never existed in her world, that's if she even looked me in the eyes. Walking by each other in halls, she ignored me completely. It was a small school, so this happened often. I wrote letters, professing my love for her, telling her I miss our friendship, and how sorry I was for being so jealous. All of them went unreturned, and I'm guessing unopened. Even her friends, who used to be my friends, gave me glares. Much of senior year was a miserable blur.

I remember focusing on a very scary thought to me, both then and now. I had wondered if the situation would have been better if she were dead. It was the first time I had ever remotely thought about someone dying. I reasoned that if she was just gone I wouldn't have to put up with the ignoring from her, and I felt that the pain would be a different one. As it was, she was there, but out of my reach. If she was dead I would have known better than to think I could ever be with her again. I realized that this was the most selfish act I could ever think of, and was a result of how hurt I was. I never specifically wished death on her, but when I think of that in terms of what happened to my wife it makes it hurt even more that I had ever once entertained that scenario.

When my wife died, sometimes during dark times, I thought of what I used to think about Abby and wishing she were dead. With my wife, I would have given anything – now, then, and forever – just to spend another moment with her. I used to go around the house, go into the closet, and just sit there taking in the smells. I used to hope that her ghost would visit me and comfort me in a way only seen in movies or you read about happening to other people.

The ghosts would come, as they did to me that night in Key West, but only in my sleep. I wanted something real, something tangible, but I only saw her figure in my dreams, and she always went the other way. If I ran faster after her, she ran faster. If I tried to sneak up on her, she was always one step ahead.

I would get angry when I thought about what I wanted with Abby in regards to what actually happened to my wife. I wondered if I had been punished for wishing death. My calmer self realized that when it came to Abby, I was just a kid that had had my heart broken. In a regretful moment of weakness I thought that if I were to throw away everything that ever reminded me of my wife it would take away some of the pain, and maybe the ghosts would stop coming to me in my dreams. After all, all of her personal effects were in a way a ghost in their own right. If I disposed of them, I reasoned, she would have no reason to hang around anymore. It didn't work, as I was once again reminded that morning when I woke up next to Bahama, hung over, and sweating in the hot room.

It had been a while since I had had the ghost dream. I tried to shake the dreams and hangover cobwebs out of my head. I rolled out of bed, sat at the desk and tried my best to hunker down and get lost in my writing. Every day for a week or so was about the same. I would wake up, take Bahama for a short walk, eat, and get down to writing. An hour or two into my writing my wife would consume all of my thoughts, making it near impossible for me to get any work done. The one thing that usually drowned out sadness – my writing – wasn't doing it anymore.

I felt I had to get out of the room. Here I was in one of the greatest walking towns in America and I was barely making it to the hallway of the bed and breakfast, let alone outside. I was beginning to feel that I was very close to going through at least another year of mourning, only this time I was in Florida and not in my own house with my parents close by.

For a week or two, it took everything I could muster to not pack up the car and drive straight back to my house. Only I had the thought, a very strong thought, that if I did that I may never leave the house again, and that over time living an agoraphobic lifestyle would have been just fine with me.

While I felt a certain amount of peace with that idea I also knew that I couldn't waste my life like that. That would be the absolute worst tribute I could give my wife. She died trying to live. I didn't want to live while waiting to die. There are multiple ways of dying, I was learning, and if I just sat around my house until that day came, then my theoretical death date on my tombstone could appear years before my heart stopped beating.

After another week of attempting to write and failing, then spending the rest of the day waiting for meals, I started going on short walks with Bahama. One of the things I spent a lot time doing during these walks was to go down to the piers and watch the boats come and go from the docks. A lot of them were fishing boats, but there were also cargo ships, party boats, and people who lived in their boats. However, I enjoyed the action of the party fishing boats the most. The tourists that got on these boats always looked a bit worried as they didn't know what to expect – perhaps fighting a fear of sea sickness. But, whenever they came back, they almost always had a large smile on their faces. Seeing them smile, particularly the kids, usually brought a smile to my face.

Back home, when I finally got outside of my house, I spent a lot of time fishing, but that was in a man-made pond, with a 12 dollar fishing pole, and worms for bait. I had never been on a big charter boat like the ones I was spying on. I wondered how much of it was a tourist trap when I first started watching the boats, but I soon realized that the enormous size of the fish that these tourists were catching was indeed real. It also turned out that a lot of them would take the fish with them, presumably to fry them up later for a tasty meal. I learned by unintentionally following one of these families back into town, that there was a nearby restaurant that would clean and cook them for you while throwing the sides in for free. If it was a particularly big fish, I later learned, the restaurant would gladly give you your meal for free, if you would give them the leftover fish. As most people were tourists, with no way to store the fish, they would gladly accept the offer of a free dinner, enjoying the fruits of their labor. The restaurant in turn could serve the freshest fish in the area – just hours out of the sea.

I walked up to the first dockside counter I could find with a sign for the Key West Party Boat Company. I realized that most people on this boat, and any other of the charter boats, would be going out with a big group of friends and family, but I wouldn't have that choice unless I wanted to ask Frank and Jean, but they were homebodies, and certainly weren't hurting for food. I was used to doing things solo, Bahama aside, so I wasn't too uncomfortable as I approached the counter inquiring about prices and times.

Keep in mind, fishing for me was merely a time-waster, and I could tell you very little about the ins-and-outs of the sport. With the pond, I knew I was catching trout mostly, because it was stocked with them a few times a year, but every now and then I would catch a fish having no idea what type it was. It was all relative to me anyway, as I always threw everything back. So, when Tommy at the Key Largo Party Fishing Boat Company told me the types of fish I could catch if I went out it was all lost on me.

"There's mackerel, a few types of snapper, yellow tail, and trigger fish, but you tourists like to catch the big groupers the most," said Tommy, wearing a tan long-sleeved T-shirt, a darker tan, and wraparound sunglasses.

They can always spot the tourists, I thought.

"When do you go out again? What do I need to bring?"

"We go out again tomorrow morning at 9, and at 2; the 9 a.m. boat is pretty subdued, usually families. The 2 p.m. is usually a little wilder, we let them bring beer, and then when they get back their party just continues down the street. As far as your other question, all you need to bring is yourself."

While I was turning into a little bit more of a drinker than usual down here in the Keys, I didn't think I could hang with a group of guys that were most likely going to party way more than I ever could. Plus, they'd all be friends. With the families I felt I could fit in a little more, or at least stay out of the way.

"I'll take the 9 a.m.," I said while handing him my credit card.

14

I started keeping my window open nearly 24 hours a day a few weeks into my stay. The cat that had caused so much disruption the first night was now a regular fixture on my bed, and came and went as it pleased. Bahama, seeing that I was cool with the situation, accepted the new visitor, and would often times lay right next to "Keysey" on the bed. When Jean told me the calico's name I sort of chuckled, thinking it little more than a play on words, when she once again educated me on something.

"Being 'keysey' is how we describe the way of life down here. In other places they may describe it as being laid back, or taking it easy, you know—just chilling out. Down here though, it's 'keysey'. As you can see," she said, pointing to Keysey, completely out of it, and sleeping on her back, "she's keysey."

During my time there, from Jean, and other locals, I learned that they absolutely detested the people who make up the imposter keysey group. It turns out that a large group of people coming to The Keys think it is okay to do nothing – opting to drink in bars and partake in drugs and walk around zoned out. Yes, they live here, technically making them locals, but the long time locals don't have these frauds in mind when they are talking about what it's like to be keysey. The real keysey ones know how to relax, but they also know how to work hard and be a meaningful member of society. Listening to some of them, you can't help but think civil war could be raged in The Keys at some point. It would be the most laid back war in the history of civilization.

I instantly liked the idea of being keysey but doing

such a touristy thing as going on a fishing boat didn't seem like such a keysey thing to do, and mentioned it to Jean.

"No, doing a party boat isn't very keysey, but you can argue working on one is. Anyway, have a nice time, and it's nice you're getting out," she said, ending the conversation on a motherly note.

After a breakfast of star fruit, and a couple of other goodies, since Jean had pretty much given me free reign of the house, I headed for the party boat.

I arrived a bit early, so I watched the boat prepare from my usual spot when I went on walks, but it was different knowing I was going to be on the boat I've spied on for a few weeks. I can't say I was nervous, but I had never gone fishing for such big fish. I hadn't weighed a fish before, but I'm guessing the biggest one I ever caught was around eight pounds. Eight pounds was about the size of the bait we would be using on the boat.

At about quarter 'til, I saw families gathering on the dock, so I headed over. In a bin attached to the outside of the office where I paid for my party boat ticket yesterday, was the most random collection of things I had ever seen. At first I thought it acted like a junk drawer, like one would have in their house, because there were hammers and wrenches, but upon closer inspection there were also broken golf clubs, knifes, fishing poles, and even a bachelor party blow-up doll. Tommy, apparently reading my thoughts, or just used to curious tourists looking in that bin, enlightened me.

"Those are just a few of the things people have caught while out on the boat. The more expensive things people have taken with them."

"It's so big out there, how often do people catch something that isn't a fish?"

Expecting the question, Tommy answered as soon as I sputtered the last syllable "More than you would think," then announced to the rest of the collection of people, "Okay, everyone onto the boat!"

After bringing the gear on and releasing us from the dock, Tommy got into the spiel he's probably told a million times. He told the adults they can wear a life-jacket if they want, but don't have to, but all the children are required by law to do so. He also introduced us to Bob, a man with long black hair and wearing a tie-dyed long sleeved shirt, and Casper, the boat's captain. All told there were about 15 of us on the party boat that morning.

When we had been cruising for about 20 minutes, Tommy began to set up the fishing rods, and started talking to the party.

"We haven't caught too many record-breakers out here, but other boats in the dock have. Now here's the rule about that – in order for the fish to be considered a record-breaker you have to catch the fish by yourself. For nearly everyone on the boat, and especially the children, that will be hard, but, if you think you have a huge one and want to try to be a record-breaker, you have to do it yourself. If me or Bob here helps you drag her in we can still take a picture and get it cooked up for you, but sadly, your name won't make it in the newspaper. Anyway, let's fish!"

There wouldn't be any record-breakers that day, but everyone on board seemed to have a lot of fun. Some of the parents and I spoke lightly between bites about how our vacations were going, our professions, and the like, but for the most part I was left alone. After reeling up a grouper that I was happy about, Tommy brought me back down to earth.

"Nice catch, but every Johnny and Jane on this

boat could have brought that guy up unassisted," while laughing at his own joke and giving me a hearty pat on the back. I laughed, and asked him how long he's been working on this boat.

"This boat particular, just a couple of months, but I've worked on all kinds of boats around the country."

"Are you like a party boat master – work for hire type deal?" I asked, also laughing at my own joke.

"Not quite like that. I have my own boat, and I like to just float around mostly wherever it takes me. Only sometimes if I float around too much I run out of food so I have to come back ashore to make money so I can do it all over again. No wife or kids, I have a few lady friends on shore here and there, but this is the life I want and wouldn't want it any other way."

A man I can relate to, I thought. Only problem was he was living it, and I was just stopping in for a visit. When I was deep into my reading of adventure stories while I was trying to get out of my funk, boating stories were always some of my favorite to read.

"Have you written about any of your adventures"? I asked, wondering if I had read anything he had written.

"I have a journal that I think about trying to get published at some point, is about it. Say, how are you enjoying your stay here? I've seen you sitting up on that dock a few times. I'm guessing you aren't a tourist, cause most tourists don't spend their time spying on boats from the dock," laughing again.

After I assured him I wasn't spying him, or anyone on the boat, and instead just passing time, I told him, "I guess I'm doing something similar to you, only in a car. Just driving around and checking out parts of the country I've never seen before, with my dog. I've liked it here so much I haven't been in a hurry to leave."

Between Tommy helping the other patrons drag fish up on to the deck, and talking to me, I explained to him that my wife died, and that I was a writer, though lately I haven't been much of a writer and that a lot of my hanging out at the piers was just my attempt at trying to break up the monotony. I was surprised at how openly I had talked about my wife's death with him. It was the second time in just a few days, when you include my late night chat with Jean. I thought me being more open was a good thing, though I still felt myself holding back on some things, afraid to open any hallways I was afraid to go down. After all, on the boat, I was a few miles away from shore. It's one thing to walk home from a bar when I start feeling badly; it's another to have to jump in the ocean to get back home.

Tommy stared out into the ocean for a minute, thinking "If you're really bored you can come work on the boat if you want. Bob here is leaving in a few days so we'll have an opening."

"That's a very nice offer, but I don't know the first thing about working on a boat," I replied.

"Well, I saw you bait your own line, that's about half the job. The other half is being a nice enough guy. You seem to have that covered too. It's very low stress, and we'll pay you under the table, though the pay will be mostly in fish," Tommy said, laughing, and then added, "If your dog's nice, she can come too."

I immediately wondered if Bahama would jump into the ocean when she saw a fish, but the walls of the boat were probably tall enough to alleviate most of those concerns. I answered, "Let me think about it. You said Bob is leaving in a few days?"

"Yup, couple days, just show up Thursday morning if you want on."

When we got back to the dock, empty handed, having just caught a few small ones and tossing them back, I walked back to my room thinking Jean will be proud of me. This was indeed very keysey of me.

15

On Thursday I started my new job. I arrived at about a quarter to nine. I came solo, which I did the entire time I worked on the boat. The thought of Bahama jumping off the side of the boat and ending up who knows where – maybe the Bahamas – was too big of a concern for me.

Tommy smiled when he saw me. "I was hoping you'd come. Welcome to the team!"

Casper gave me a slight nod from the wheel, and said, "Welcome aboard, matey."

"Should I get here earlier, I wasn't sure?" I asked.

"You can if you want, but I won't dock your pay if you don't show up till later," laughing, he continued. "I get here about an hour before we head out just to get things going, if you want to help, cool, if not, no worries, matey."

"Oh. Okay." Feeling nervous, I stared out into the water.

"Remember what Bob did a couple days ago? He just went around being friendly and asking if anyone needs help when they got a bite? If any of the little ones need help with their life vests or anyone asks for a drink, there's a cooler in the back. They are free – they should be for as much as we charge them to go fishing for a few hours. That's all I really need you to do. If you have any other questions when we are out there, just let me know."

Quickest training I ever received for any job, but, then again, I hadn't had a "real" job since college—if pizza delivery is considered a real job, that is.

We pulled away from the dock. Tommy told me that I would only be doing the 9 a.m. because they had a full crew for the 2 p.m. That was fine with me because I didn't want Bahama's entire day to be cramped in the room. Also, it gave me time to write before it got too late, should I have chosen to write.

The group was very similar to the 9 a.m. boat I had done just a couple of days earlier, lots of families of three to six, vacationing, and hoping to catch Moby Dick, or at least catch a big one to take a family photo with to put back on their office desk in Real World, U.S.A.

My first trip out was pretty uneventful. Most of the time I helped children bait their hooks when the parents didn't want anything to do with it, or know how. Being a novice myself, I had many of the children laughing at my futile efforts, despite Tommy showing me how to do it properly more than once. Most of the bait, to me anyway, just seemed like smaller versions of the fish that the tourists were trying to catch. It was obvious to everyone on board, including Tommy, that I was ignorant to just about anything to do with fishing, but luckily they didn't care that much.

About halfway through the trip, one of the father tourists on the trip brought up a decent-sized grouper. He had no desire to keep it, and was about to toss it back over board when I saw Tommy stop him. Tommy put the fish in a giant cooler located in the center of the boat, while explaining to the father tourist that groupers are one of the hardest fish to reel on board, and that it was a small miracle that he did it so easily by himself. Grouper, I learned from Tommy, and later watching others drag them in, dart around frantically, smacking against the boat repeatedly. It's not uncommon for it to take 30 seconds to bring it to the side of the boat, but ten minutes to drag it in. This didn't explain why Tommy wanted to keep the fish, but I didn't think much of it.

In a lull in action, Captain Casper gave me a rundown of the best places to catch specific types of fish, most of which I forgot immediately. He said the grouper we caught was native to a group of reefs where not many of the other party boats go. He said he usually goes to this place because most people just want the thrill of catching a fish and having to fight a bit for it. For some of the afternoon partiers, those that are just treating this as a respite until they can get to Duval, he heads out into the ocean. The bites are fewer, but the partiers hardly notice, but when they catch one it can be one of many types of fish, delighting them. I was beginning to feel sorry I wouldn't get to be a part of the rowdier groups that hunt for the more exciting types of fish, but was happy to learn a solid lesson from Casper.

When we got back to the dock, I helped the guys hose off the deck, and restock the bait for the next session, taking off in less than an hour from when we got back. When I was getting ready to head back to Jean's, Tommy stopped me, holding the grouper he had saved.

"You know where O'Riley's Place is, the restaurant around the corner?" he asked. I remembered this was the restaurant I had watched the family go to with their catch unintentionally.

"Yup, pass by it almost every day. Is this where this guy is heading?" I asked while pointing to the fish.

"You got it. Bring this over there, go in the back door, and give it to whomever the cook is today, probably Seymour. Tell him to cook it up for us and have it ready at 7; tell him we want his famous sandwiches. You'll meet me there?"

"Yeah. See ya then."

"You can bring your dog too. They have outside seating, plus I'm guessing she'll like what we're having."

"Great, she'll like that."

I went over to O'Riley's Place, handed the fish off to a large Samoan man with a bigger knife, giving him the specific directions from Tommy. Seymour smiled and said, "No problem," and went back to work just as quickly.

When I got back to the room, Bahama gave me a curious face after she smelled me. She wasn't used to me smelling like fish, but, like Tommy had said, I was guessing she'd like her meal later tonight. I showered, and threw my clothes into the hamper, realizing that I would have to do a lot more laundry if I didn't want my room to smell like rotted fish. Unfortunately, Jean did all the laundry, so I would have to talk to her about maybe doing my laundry every day. After drying off, I went downstairs to find her, and asked about paying a little more per week in turn for more laundry service.

"You're working on the fishing boat now right? I'm guessing you'll have quite a few opportunities of bringing me some fresh fish?"

"You got it." That was easy enough. For the duration of my stay she began adding some fish courses to the nightly dinner.

After taking care of Jean, or, more appropriately, Jean taking care of me, I went back to the room for a while and got some writing in before announcing to Bahama it was time to go. With a cocked head, she jumped on the bed and waited for me to put on her collar and leash.

I met Tommy at O'Riley's, getting there just a few minutes before he did, smelling doubly as fishy as I had, having worked two shifts. The smell of fresh meats cooking inside the restaurant drowned out that smell, and any other smell that may have been dragged in off the city's streets and boats.

We ordered beers and a bowl of water for Bahama. Bahama wasn't as interested in the water as she was in Tommy, or more particularly his fishy smell. Tommy didn't seem to mind Bahama jumping in his lap, but I thought Tommy would probably like to enjoy his meal without a hound under his chin. I picked up Bahama and sat her down on the other side of me.

He asked me how I thought my first day went, and other small talk, but it was clear we were both just waiting for food. After a long bout of silence, I asked if he knew the history of the restaurant or if he had met O'Riley himself. After laughing at that question, he told me nobody knew O'Riley, and it was most likely that this restaurant was originally opened as a drug front, saying they fudged the books for this place in order to make money at their real jobs. He explained that's at least how it started, but the food here was so good that it became a must-eat for locals. Tommy told me that many restaurants in the Keys claim to have "The Best Grouper Sandwich in the Keys." Tommy told me they are all lying, "The best one is here." A few minutes later I got my first taste.

Having never eaten a grouper sandwich before I had nothing to compare it to, but it didn't matter. By default then it was the best grouper sandwich I had ever eaten, but it was also one of the best meals I ever had. In addition to the sandwich, I had french-fries and a vegetable mix, though the latter hardly got touched.

When we were finishing up, Seymour came out of the back and put a pack, the rest of the grouper, in front of Tommy. Tommy thanked him, and asked him if he kept some for himself, which he had. Tommy handed the pack to me.

"I wasn't joking when I said you would be paid in fish," he said, chuckling. He wasn't lying though— that was how I was paid my month I worked on the boat. That worked out just fine, as that is exactly how I paid Jean, in part, my last month there.

16

The fresh air on the boat restored me a great deal. I began writing again, and at a pretty good clip. The remaining weeks in Key West ran together, but at a perfect pace. I woke up, I fished, I wrote, I ate. I'm guessing that set-up would be perfect for most men, save the writing part. I truly loved it there, and could see myself spending many more days there – both then and in the future – but I was beginning to think it was time to go.

There was no situation or person, other than me, that had made the decision that it was time. A lot of times when I was sitting idly in the room, or walking around town, I started thinking that my time in the Keys was not unlike how I spent my time back home in Virginia. Sure, I had never worked on a fishing boat in Virginia, but the monotony of everyday began to remind me of how I reacted when my wife died, so in return it reminded me of her death. One of the worst things I figured I could do was to begin to associate such a wonderful place, with such a horrible thought as her demise. I had never been within 400 miles of the Florida Keys with my wife, but when a thought caught my mind, I had learned, it was pretty much there to stay.

Additionally, while I thought that I was beginning to be introduced with a story that I thought would make for a good read, I felt like on paper my story was starting to get a little boring. Don't get me wrong, drinking where Hemingway drank, and writing where he wrote, however inconsistent, are memories I'll never forget, and always be glad I have, but I originally sought out to have a grand adventure. I knew it would have been very easy for me to get into a long, perhaps lifelong, routine in the Keys, one I would have enjoyed very much, but in my mind that wasn't the point of this trip.

When I first decided I was leaving, I started thinking where could I go that was the exact opposite of the Keys. I didn't mean somewhere 20 below zero; I meant the opposite of "keysey." It didn't take me long before I knew exactly where I was heading. It would be a long drive, but I believed I had a strong enough grasp on geography to think much of the drive would be rather easy. Also, unlike the Keys, I wouldn't have to worry about rain.

A few days before I left, I went to tell Jean the news. She was in the kitchen preparing a dinner with some of the grouper I had brought her just a few hours before. The news wasn't really surprising to her.

"I knew you were leaving here soon," she told me.

"How'd you know that"?

"I could just tell you were getting a little restless is all."

I knew she was a lot like my mother. "Well, you guys have been nothing but kind to me, and I'm really going to miss it here."

"Just 'cause you're leaving doesn't mean we don't think you'll come back. We'll keep a bed turned for you," she smiled.

"You know, Jean, you make it really hard to leave."

When I told Tommy I was leaving soon, he told me he was getting ready to head back out on his own boat as well.

"Looks like old Casper here is going to have to find a couple more vagabonds in a few days," he said nodding in the direction to Casper, during one of my last trips out to sea.

On my last outing, Tommy gave me two large grouper as my last payment, which I promptly deposited into Jean's freezer. The circle of life.

When I began packing the night before we left, I began feeling sad I was leaving, but was ready to get to where I was getting. Bahama, who had learned to associate a suitcase with a ride the way she associated a leash with a walk, was also ready to go. The cat on the bed looked at me questioningly when I first got out the suitcase, then turned over and went back to sleep. I briefly entertained the idea of traveling with a cat and dog, but just as quickly dismissed it. Besides, Keysey would have no trouble making friends with the next occupants of my room. I hoped Jean would at least remind the next guests that Keysey may just decide 2 a.m. is a good time to introduce herself to the new guests.

The next morning I felt melancholy, but still felt my time in the Keys was done. Better to leave a day early than a day late my dad told me on the phone that morning.

I stuck around long enough to have another one of Jean's breakfasts, spent a little time petting the cat while Bahama looked on jealously, and hit the road.

As I hit the door, Jean reminded me once more that I'd always have a room there, and for the first time questioned where I was going.

"Where are you heading anyway?" she asked.

I turned back into the house one more time, smiling.

"Vegas, baby!"

17

Despite never embarking on a journey this long, I followed the directions fairly easily. First it's straight up the map for 400 miles, or so, and then left for 2,100 more. I considered heading 520 miles north instead of 400 just to get another BBQ sandwich from The GA Pig Shack, but Jean made me a few grouper sandwiches that would get me through the first few hundred miles of the trip.

Passing by Kona Kai, I briefly entertained the idea of stopping, but even coming close to creating another scene like we did on our initial visit was enough to keep me driving, regardless of how pretty Becky was.

I was going to take this drive pretty leisurely. I didn't have any must-see places lined up, despite driving nearly the entire length of the country. It really didn't matter to me if I made it in three days, or four days, or even five. But, for the sake of Bahama, and her little legs, I hoped to make decent time.

Driving had always been therapeutic for me, which made me wonder why I didn't drive at all for nearly a year after my wife died. Some of it was me being against pretty much anything outside of my four walls, but I think a lot of it reminded me of when I first met my wife.

Throughout high school, Abby had consumed most of my life. She was what I considered my first love for the remainder of high school, despite breaking up prior to senior year. I went on what I guess would be described as dates with other girls during that time, but most were group affairs with friends, and looking back on it now, I can't remember any of those girls names without really straining my brain. I went to a small school, too.

I was able to concentrate enough through my fogged mind to get decent grades and even earned a partial scholarship to a school in Virginia even farther south than where I already lived. New River University was known through the state of Virginia where you went when you couldn't get into a better four-year university. In reality, the school ranked in the middle of the pack in terms of education, but its reputation as a party school outweighed the educational value any outsiders saw in it.

My guess to why it became a party school is because there isn't anything else to do, unless you fancy cowtipping. But honestly, who does that more than once? Or twice?

The city was a simple one to master in about an hour. New River University made up 80 percent of the city's confines. The university was right in the middle. On the left and right of the university buildings were neighborhoods. When school was in session the city reached a population of about 15,000, when it was summer vacation it dwindled to about 7,500. Also, on nearly all sides of the school were one or two convenient stores. My business teacher once told our class that the 7-Eleven to the left of campus sold more beer than any other store in Virginia, and ranked in the top 50 beer sales in the country. The Quick-E-Mart on the right side of campus wasn't far behind, at fourth. Keep in mind only 7,500 residents were there year round.

In front of the campus was our modest main street, aptly named, "Main Street." On the surface it looked like any Main Street in Small Town U.S.A., but our mile long street was lined with bars. The bars must have come upon an agreement a long time ago on who got dibs on what night each bar would have their special weekly promotion. For example, if you went to Billy's on a Tuesday night you would be lucky if you got in the door, and if you did get in the door you would most likely be squished against a wall. Still, Billy's held the monopoly on Tuesday nights in New River. However, if you went there on a Wednesday, you were likely to have the place to yourself. My friends and I eventually learned to choose Billy's on Wednesday because of that reason.

My first day on campus, a few days before my freshman year started, I went with my friend Drew to get our books. There were two places we could get our books – the actual university bookstore or the used bookstore. I chose the university bookstore because my partial scholarship would render these books free. It also turned out to be the best decision I ever made.

We walked into the store, and like Billy's on a Tuesday night, it was packed. Drew was talking to me about how much beer we were going to drink and how many chicks we were going to bag during our stay on campus, but when I saw her, he could have been telling me the most profound thing in the world and I still wouldn't have heard a word he was saying. My future wife was looking overwhelmed in her university provided uniform as she attempted to keep up with the ever-growing crowd. In one instant she was helping someone at the register, and the very next she was running to help another student in an aisle across the store.

I thought she was beautiful. Her brownish-red hair was in a bun, and her shirt was partially untucked. Her jeans fit amazingly though. She always laughed when I told her I thought she was the most beautiful thing I ever saw the first time I saw her, reminding me that on that day she was sweaty, tired, and in a less than flattering university polo shirt, but I would ignore her argument and I asked instead if she still had those jeans.

I can remember to this day how Drew continuing to talk while I just stared at him as to ask him if he didn't realize what was going on here. No, he was oblivious; Drew was still fantasizing about his future campus hi-jinks. At least I thought he was; I still wasn't listening, fantasizing myself.

I must have run into a dozen people keeping an eye on her while I went around and gathered my books. I was hoping she would get called to cash register duty just so I could stand within a few feet of her. Even then I knew I wouldn't talk to her, other than the please and thank you's that take place during a typical customer-cashier exchange. I did indeed come up unlucky during that first trip to the bookstore, but before I even left that day I knew I would be looking for any excuse to come back, and as soon as possible.

Drew and I got back to our dorm room, and despite being an occupant of that dorm room for less than three hours, I already knew I hated dorm room living. First of all, the entire building smelled like it used to produce dog food. Secondly, it seemed that everyone in the building, on all six floors, was in a competition to see who could play their music the loudest. Coming from a house where I always had my own room, and a ruckus was considered our dog barking, I knew this would be tough. That first night I can still remember sipping on a beer from a case Drew had secured for us, not really drinking it because honestly how many 18 year olds really like beer by then? By the end of freshman year I liked beer just fine.

As I finally drifted off to sleep that night I was already having deep, intellectual conversations, with my future wife. The one I hadn't even spoken to yet.

The next day I woke up, went to the dining hall and had some runny eggs, and made up some lie to Drew about forgetting a book at the store yesterday. I secretly hoped Drew would not want to join me, and he obliged. Drew was one of the few 18 year olds who genuinely liked beer, and drank early and often. Because of that habit, he lasted only a year on campus, but he was far from the first one to see his time at college cut short because of partying. Last I heard he was working at his father's farm and feed store, but doing well.

While Drew went off for an early morning drink back in the room, while waiting for the bars to open, I went back to my future wife. As luck would have it, she was working and not nearly as busy as the day before, because it was still early. Totally unprepared, she walked up to me almost as soon as I walked in the store, smiling.

"Is there anything I can help you with?"

I spoke the words of all men caught off guard talking to a beautiful girl.

"Ummmm."

Then I lied.

"I need a book for my English class."

"I'd be happy to help you with that, which class?"

Now I was in a corner, having already bought the book. I figured I can always return it the next day. For the second time in two days I bought a book for the same class.

"101, Dr. Boff."

"Oh cool, I have that class too!"

Jackpot!

"Cool, I will see you there."

After taking me to the book, and handing it to me, she directed me to the cashier. That would be all I would be seeing her that day. I was bad at this.

The next day I returned hoping to both see her and not see her, so I could return my book in a non-embarrassing manner.

"Hey, it's you again! Are you stalking me?" she joked, I hoped.

Well, yes.

"No, turns out I had this book already."

"Hmmm, well that's unfortunate; let me help you with that," she said with knowing eyes.

She went up to the register, gave me a refund, and before handing me the receipt wrote something on it. Probably just a note telling her co-workers that I had returned the book in case I tried to return another one.

This moment became a crucial part of our history, because I may have just gone back every day to see her without ever taking an initiative. Luckily, my future wife wasn't a chicken like me.

"Maybe I can see you outside of my work next time," she said smiling and then walked back towards the sales floor. After staring at her as she walked away for a little too long, I looked down to the receipt to see her phone number, and a note:

"I'll see you in class, if you REALLY even have that class," with a big smiley face. Then followed that with her phone number.

Her smiley face drawing was nowhere near as big as the one on my face as I walked out the door and back across campus. My semester was made and I hadn't even had my first class yet.

18

I didn't call her because I would see her in class the next day. That, and because I was a chicken. I wondered if she thought this would be a slight and that I wasn't interested, which couldn't be farther from the truth. It wasn't an easy decision, as I really wanted to call her about 10 minutes after she gave me her number. And I thought about it every 10 minutes for the remainder of the day. Still, by this point I had caught Drew up to speed about my bookstore crush, and he told me that if I called her too soon it would seem desperate. I believe guys have been telling each other that line since the beginning of time.

I arrived to class early that first day, even before Dr. Boff. This caused me to panic again because I feared that my future wife would come in next and I wouldn't know what to say to her. Luckily, she came in the middle of the pack, and took a seat on the opposite side of the room of me. It would be the last time we were ever that far apart, assuming we were in the same room together.

I tested my peripheral vision with everything that first class. For a million dollars, I couldn't have recalled one complete sentence that Professor Boff said that day. Instead I spent the whole time trying to stare at the bookstore beauty while at the same time hoping and wondering if she was looking at me. It felt like middle school.

When the hour and a half class concluded, I was debating on making a mad dash for the door, or talking to her. She made the decision for me.

While playfully punching me on the arm, and holding a smile on her face, she asked, "Why didn't you call me last night?"

"I, well, I didn't know the protocol because you had just given me your number and..."

"You're going to give me that line; I bet one of your friends told you that, huh? Ask him how many girlfriends he has had."

I couldn't remember Drew ever having a girlfriend. She was good.

"Try again tonight. My last class is over at four, I'll be expecting your call."

Once again I watched her walk away a little too long, and then I walked back to the dorm with a smile as wide as the campus.

I called her that night. The next time Dr. Boff's class met she took the seat behind me, and then the next class after that she took the seat next to me. We became inseparable from there on out.

I can't even remember the exact second we decided we would become "boyfriend and girlfriend." Neither of us believed in labels, which was the cool thing in college, but I usually thought of it as the first time we kissed.

It was a few weeks after we started seeing each other, and despite being early September, it was unseasonably cold. We were going to Billy's because it was a Tuesday night, and that's what you did as a freshman of New River University. Plus, they didn't check ID, which was just fine for my buddy Drew.

Everyone walked in New River. You partially walked because there was a decent chance you were drinking when you went out, but also because the farthest away anything was worth going to was still less than a mile.

My future wife met Drew and I in our dorm room. Drew always took forever to get ready – combing his hair, changing his shirt six times, between pulls on his bottle of beer. Because Drew had already started pre-gaming, he had grown a bit unfocused.

Finally we left, and within a few minutes we had one of our first "firsts." We held hands. I wasn't sure if it was a product of it being so cold, or if we had reached that point in our relationship, but I didn't care either way. When we got to Billy's there was a bit of a line, but after a wait of about five minutes we were one with the others in the swarm of bodies, and on our way to the bar for our I.D. free beers.

At least that was our intent. Instead, after standing in a line that appeared to only get longer, I backed away from the line. I attempted to talk to my date, but because of the music being so loud everything resulted in a scream. I could tell she wasn't having a good time. I was going to stay, not knowing for sure if she wanted to and being that I had came with Drew, but my mind was made up when she leaned into me and screamed.

"YOU WANT TO GET OUT OF HERE? THIS IS RIDICULOUS!"

I made a half-hearted attempt to find Drew to let him know we were leaving, but it was impossible in the sea of people. I also knew with their quarter beer special he would have stayed anyway.

Without saying another word, I grabbed her hand and went back out into the chilly night. We briefly discussed the idea of going to another bar knowing that it would be nearly empty because Tuesday's was Billy's night, but I was glad when she didn't show much of an interest. The prospect of walking around the quiet town and campus alone was too much to pass up, I remember thinking to myself. She later told me she was thinking the same thing.

During the course of our walk I learned that her

parents had become upset knowing that she was spending time with "some boy" despite only being a university student for a few weeks. I was taken aback by the comment, but during that same conversation learned that her older sister had quit college to chase "some boy" and after getting married at 19, she was divorced at 20, after a physically abusive relationship which saw her in the hospital twice. They didn't want the same thing for their other daughter, and I could respect that. I promised to her that night that it was not my intention, nor would it ever be my intention to stop her from doing what she wanted to accomplish in her life, which was to be a veterinarian. She later told me that that line from me went a long way into knowing I was a good guy. While the line helped her, and in turn my chances with her, it took a bit longer to impress her parents.

That was also the first time I ever told her about Abby. She had never had a serious boyfriend, being afraid to upset her parents after witnessing the hardships that her older sister went through, six years her senior.

"College years are for trying and exploring new things. Didn't your guidance counselor tell you that?" I joked.

She unclasped my hand just to give me another punch on the arm, sliding her hand back into mine. I was already more comfortable with her than I ever had been with Abby, and I knew there would be none of this "on again off again" foolishness with her.

As Tuesday turned to Wednesday, we were making our second trek around campus when we stopped at a playground right on the edge of campus that was built for the children in the surrounding neighborhoods, though nobody could ever remember seeing an actual child play on it.

We sat down at the bottom of the slide, barely wide enough for us both to fit, with suited me perfectly. It was during this time I really looked at her, with the guidance of a street light giving her the perfect spotlight, though she always seemed to glow anyways. Her green eyes were always so full of emotion, and I learned to tell what kind of mood she was in just by looking in them for a few seconds. Her hair was up, but in a more stylish way she had it while working. I mentioned her freckles on her slim cheeks and she told me she hated them, but she used to have many more when she was a child. I loved them.

We must have sat there for an hour, gradually getting colder, but gradually snuggling deeper and deeper into each other. I had been secretly hoping that this would be the night that we would kiss. I also learned later that she wanted to kiss me just the same, but after taking the initiative to give me her phone number, she had made the decision that the ball was now in my court.

I was both enjoying our time together, but beginning to get upset with myself as I failed to kiss her. Finally, after what must have been another 20 minutes of battling back in forth in my mind on if I should or shouldn't, I gathered all the strength I had, and kissed her while she was in the middle of a sentence telling me about her childhood dog. I didn't make a habit of interrupting her during our relationship, but that was more than worth it. After a few seconds I leaned away, and gauged her reaction. Her eyes seemed surprised, but also told me she didn't mind. She didn't mind. The next kiss, which she called our first real kiss because she was involved in the entire process, saw her meet me half way. To me, that's when we became girlfriend and boyfriend.

19

It turns out that she hated dorm living just as much as me. After our freshman year on campus we both found apartments with roommates though my place acted as little more than a storage unit, because I spent nearly every night at her nicer place. My parents knew that I was exclusively staying at her house fairly early on because I never felt the need to lie about those things to my parents. I could tell that they weren't thrilled with that news but at the same time they understood that we really liked each other.

Her parents were an entirely different story. After our sophomore year, we got our own place together. My wife to be never told her parents we lived together.

Luckily, at least in this instance, her parents made only a couple of trips a year down to the college, but when they did it was always a humorous scene for our friends. When we got word her parents were coming to visit we immediately went into making her apartment look like it was occupied by her and her only. I gathered up all my clothes, video games, DVD's and even my computer, and stored them at the house I had lived in, since I still knew the guys who lived there.

Additionally, we had parties in our apartment from time to time, so I had to take all the beer and liquor out of the house as well. Her parents were very anti-drinking, attributing drinking to their older daughter's thought process while she was in college. The guys at my old apartment didn't care about my belongings being there, but as a penalty for taking up space they thought it only fair that they could drink all the alcohol I brought over. This was an unspoken agreement, as I had never agreed to it, but I understood. My choices were limited. I was just glad her parents didn't come to visit more often.

My wife had met my family at the end of our first year together, and everything went well, as I expected. It was there that I saw her in a family setting for the first time, and loved how natural it was for her to get along with my parents and my older sister. She looked like she was right at home. I literally remember seeing her in a different light both figuratively and literally as I watched her have an easy going conversation at our family dining room table, as the sun came in through our deck door. Seeing her get along with my family so easily made me like her even more. Because of this, and Abby becoming a figment of my imagination, I thought I knew what love was for the first time.

Now here I was, getting ready to meet her parents just a few weeks after our sophomore year started. Through the course of that summer I didn't get to see her because she was still afraid to tell her parents just how serious our relationship was. While I could sympathize with her being torn, I have to admit it made me upset too. It was clear that she spent a lot of time on the phone talking to me. In learning more about me, through her, she said it seemed her parents were beginning to warm up to the idea of me and maybe even realized I wasn't as bad as they had thought.

So, after cleaning out the apartment of any sign of me, her parents made their visit. I can remember putting on this big production just prior to them getting there, and lasting throughout their visit. I left our apartment and drove around for a bit until her parents got there. She then called me to "invite" me over, and a few minutes later I was entering my own apartment as a visitor.

If entering as a visitor wasn't awkward enough, I was met with a steely glance from her mother and a stiff handshake from her father. When I had left just a few minutes before, I remember the apartment being a cooler temperature. Upon reentering the house, I was now sweating like I had just finished a marathon in the Sahara.

They were sitting on the couch with my wife to be in the middle, looking like the perfect sitcom family. I chose to sit in a rickety old chair we had purchased from Goodwill that I had never sat in before. To my wife's credit she tried to start a conversation, and occasionally her dad jumped in with a question for me, about me, but her mom just sat with a forced smile and nodded her head occasionally. After about 30 minutes of that her father suggested heading out for dinner, which sounded like the greatest idea ever. The room was getting nothing but hotter.

Dinner wasn't much better. We went to a Shoney's, one of the few chain restaurants near our school, which is combined with one of the few hotels near our school. While I was relieved to be getting out of the house, I realized on the short drive that this meal wasn't going to be much better. I had only been this ridiculously nervous one time in my life, and that was before a high school homecoming dance with Abby. I had saved up every dollar for half a year wanting to impress my date with a fancy dinner. I remember hoping the ambiance of the restaurant impressed her, but I had no idea about the food personally. I didn't eat a bite.

The ambience at Shoney's didn't meet that of the restaurant with Abby, but I made sure I did my part by eating next to nothing. Between half-hearted attempts at three of the four of us starting conversation, I realized that her parents were most likely paying for the meal and I didn't want to appear rude by not eating anything. I was drinking a ton of water because my sweats had followed me inside the restaurant, but I didn't think drinking gallons of tap water would make up for the price of my sirloin and potatoes. I played with my food a little, attempting to take a bite of steak here or there, but with my throat as dry as it was I might as well have been trying to eat a bag of sand.

The only time her mom spoke to me the entire course of the evening is when she asked me if I was going to get a doggy bag, letting me know without saying it that she wasn't happy I wasn't eating. I smiled forcefully, the theme of the evening, and told her, "But of course."

Gratefully, my wife, who was always blessed with a good sense of timing, told her parents that she had a test to study for so she should head back to her place and study before going to bed. She knew they would respond to her saying she had to study. She all but winked at me when telling her parents this. She was saving me from losing another ten pounds of water weight, among other things.

When we got back to her place, her parents made sure to wait around to make sure I was leaving before they left. I finally got the hint, and realized the sooner they left the sooner I could come back. I exchanged a sweaty palm handshake with her father and a nod to her mom, and basically ran out the door so I could run to my car and blast the air conditioning. Ten minutes later she called me to say her parents had mercifully left. After driving around the parking lot for another ten minutes just to make sure they weren't sticking around to see if I was coming back, I finally parked. When I walked back into the house, my doggy bag in hand, the air was blissfully cooler and no longer thick. I took out my steak and started eating it on the spot as my wife watched me and laughed. I was starving.

20

By our senior year of college, my relationship with my wife's parents was becoming better. After three years of awkward visits her parents realized at the very least I wasn't going anywhere and at best realized their daughter was happy and doing well in school. In fact, she made the Dean's List all but one semester after an algebra class her sophomore year caused a "C." I'm sure her parents blamed this on our early relationship when their daughter broke the news of the C, but the fact was we were both bad at math.

Another defining moment in our relationship came when we found out that she would have to be heading even farther south to North Carolina to go to graduate school because New River was cancelling its veterinary program. This school, Hickory College, was even smaller than New River, but offered a great vet program that included an entire farm on its campus. I never understood why horses were so instrumental in becoming a vet, because after completing her Master's degree I don't think she ever touched another horse again.

When my wife to be got accepted into Hickory a few months into our senior year at New River, she decided to wait until her parents came to visit to tell them. To me and her, it was so clear that I would be heading to Hickory with her that the topic never even came up between us. It was just fact. However, her parents didn't share the same thoughts.

"Well, you certainly have an exciting time in your life coming up, and this will be a good opportunity for both of you to meet new people. I'm sure you'll miss each other, but you'll be so busy with your new lives…" her dad said, suggesting this would be the end of our relationship.

Without missing a beat my future wife said, "No, he's coming too. He already found a job and an apartment close to campus."

While I smiled, her parents seemed to be at a loss for words. Her mom simply said, "That's nice."

At first thought it wouldn't seem that this exchange would be so important in our history, but to me it was everything. It was one of the first times that she had ever professed her need and desire to be around me in front of her parents. If I considered our first kiss on the slide the moment we became boyfriend and girlfriend, I considered this moment as the one we became something even deeper. I realized I wanted us to be forever.

That was all well and good, but as I was quickly learning, a woman liked something a little more official than an exchange of words. The teen I had known that was so against labels was now looking for the ultimate label – married. I figured she initiated our relationship with a phone number on a book store receipt; the least I could do was solidify our relationship with a diamond ring.

In order to do that, one has to have money. Much to my wife's surprise I decided to get a paying job our final semester, instead of the editing I had been doing at the school's paper, *The New River Times*. I had already trained the next guy in line on how to do the job, and if I stuck around for the final semester it would be as little more than a figurehead. Not being a figurehead for *The New River Times* wasn't going to break my heart, so I began my next job as a pizza delivery driver. It was for a local joint that I suspected could have had an owner with a much higher investment in another illegal business, though I could never confirm this. All he needed to tell me was that the pay was under the table and I would bring home cold hard cash every night.

I suspected that most of the deliveries would be between the store and the five dorms on campus. For the most part this was true, but not as much as I suspected. It turned out that we delivered up to 15 miles away. The majority of people who lived this far away were Amish. I learned that Amish folk tipped better than any other group of people that I had the privilege of delivering to those during those three or four months. I always suspected that having very little access to the outside world was the main cause of this, as they most likely didn't know what was standard. Luckily, for me at least, they had heard of tipping.

However, they were also some of the nicest people I have ever encountered, often times inviting me into their house for a minute or so if it was cold. If it was raining they would hand me a towel to dry off and apologize for having me stand in the rain, though most times it was usually for only a few seconds. After all, I'm pretty sure it was pretty easy to tell when their pizza was coming as I was generally the only car for miles when I was in that part of town. I loved making these deliveries because the tips were almost always great and the drive would sometimes take upwards of an hour because of the slower speed limit back towards their communities.

I didn't have a date in mind when I wanted to get engaged, instead waiting for my bank account to determine the date. By the time we left New River, I hadn't made enough yet because we had spent a sizable portion of my earnings on the move and getting a new apartment. When we moved to Hickory, with my new degree in hand, I landed a job as an assistant editor at the local paper. In reality I think my pizza job paid better, but working for the *Hickory Herald* would surely make for better resume filler in the future, I reasoned. After a few months of editing stories on small town politicians and local business owners I had enough to buy an engagement ring that I felt appropriate.

I knew very little about wedding rings, so I went with what I knew about my wife to be at that time. She was a big fan of princess movies growing up, like most little girls, so when I heard the jeweler mention princess cut, I agreed. I also knew she liked white gold based on her other pieces of jewelry, so that was a must. Finally, I was pretty sure she liked diamonds, like 99.9 percent of her kind on the planet, so naturally that was the final, but most important, requirement.

The town of Hickory had exactly one jewelry store, and being too impatient to wait to buy a ring in a bigger city, I chose Dominique's Diamonds smack dab in the middle of Hickory's Main Street, not unlike that of New River's Main Street. When I walked in, an immaculately dressed old man, who I was guessing was not Dominique, paid me little attention. When he found out I had $3,000 in my left jeans pocket, he took me a little more seriously.

21

Keeping a secret has never been one of my strong qualities. For example, a few weeks before my sister's 16th birthday my parents told my sister some fib about what they were doing and went out car shopping for her. Because my sister had some plans, she was unable to babysit me, so I went along with my parents. Multiple times on the drive to the car dealership they told me I couldn't tell my sister a word about the car, because, of course, it was a surprise for her birthday. I told them I wouldn't.

After my parents picked out a nice, used, reliable automobile – a Ford four door of some sort that was about eight years old – they stored it in their friend's garage a few miles from our house. From the short ride from that garage to our house, I remember thinking I was going to burst if I didn't tell her the secret. At the age of 12 I hadn't yet comprehended that I could possibly be ruining a big surprise for her. I just wanted to tell her she was getting a car. I think I thought this would mean we would get along better. I knew she thought of me as the bratty little brother that I was, but I always looked up to her as kids and by telling her the secret I felt we would grow closer, even though in hindsight we we're pretty close already.

I briefly considered locking myself in my bedroom until her birthday surprise was delivered, but with three weeks to go until her birthday, I figured I'd get hungry. Plus, more importantly, the only television with cable was in the family room. When she came home that evening I nearly burst through my door and down the stairs to greet her.

When my parents told us to run upstairs and get ready for dinner I followed her like white on rice, nearly tripping her up the stairs. Of course, this annoyed her, but when I slid into the room just narrowly missing the door she was attempting to slam in my face, she knew something was up.

"I got a secret," holding out the first "e" for about three seconds.

"That's great, what could you possibly know that I would care about," she answered in the way teenagers spoke at that time.

"But this one's good. I promise"

"Okay, spill it."

Wanting to really tell her, but enjoying the brief upper hand in our game of "I know something you don't know," I answered, "What's in it for me?"

She replied, "Nevermind then. I don't care," and began heading for the door.

"Okay. Wait. Mom and Dad got you a car for your birthday, but you can't tell I told."

Trying to suppress her excitement from turning into a roar and alerting our parents, she asked details about the car, but all I could tell her at the time was the color. Before we went back down for dinner I asked her three more times in about 12 seconds to not tell our parents.

Little did I know that the main topic at dinner that night would be my sister's report card. Specifically, how bad it was. I was only halfway paying attention, planning in my head my evening activity, which was either watch TV or play with my Ninja Turtle action figures, when the conversation got a bit louder. Still, I never expected this next exchange.

"If you keep talking to us like that young lady we will seriously reconsider you having your birthday party here."

Then in the ultimate act of brother-sister back stabbing my sister replied, "I already know you got me a car, so don't even try it."

Stunned, I dropped my fork onto the plate as I watched three pairs of eyes fall on me. Thanks, sis.

She still got the car and birthday party, and I don't recall anything happening to me punishment wise, but it was the last time I remembered anyone telling me a secret. About 10 years after attempting to keep a secret from my sister, I now had my future wife's engagement ring in my pocket. With age, I hadn't gotten any better with secrets.

Despite how much I wanted to blurt out to my future wife what I had purchased and propose I held out for something I figured was a little romantic. Plus, from our talks I knew that the proper thing in her family was for me to ask her father for permission before I popped the question. If my homecoming dance and meeting her parents were number one and two on my all-time list of nerve producing things I had done, this came in a close third.

The day after I bought the ring, she had gone to class, leaving me alone in our apartment with my cell phone and a very important phone call on my mind. I waited until I thought her dad would surely be at work because I didn't want her mother to not only be there, but listen in. Talking to just her dad would be nerve-wracking enough. Through the few years my wife and I had been dating my relationship with her father had gotten better. It turned out we had some things in common, including a love for reading anything we could get our hands on. That usually provided us enough to talk about during those increasingly less awkward meetings with her parents.

I didn't take nearly as long as I thought I would to pull up the courage to make the call. I knew that I wanted to marry her, and this was just another step to get to that goal. He answered the phone on the first ring, quicker than I expected, but still I wasted no time getting into the reason I called for fear I would pass out.

"Hello, sir, I called to ask for your daughter's hand in marriage."

"Okay, do you want her whole body in marriage, or just her hand?" He asked. I was so put off by the question I didn't know how to handle it, hardly noticing this was his attempt at a joke. Instead, I asked the question more clearly, or as clearly as I could at that point.

"No. I. Um. I wanted to ask your permission to make sure I had your blessing in marrying your daughter."

"What if I said no?"

My heart dropped. If I wouldn't have been already sitting on the couch, I would have dropped too.

"Well, um…" Then I heard him break into a laughter which at that moment was one of the best things I had ever heard.

"Ha, ha, ha! I really got you; you must have been sweating as bad as the first time you met us!" I hadn't realized our relationship had reached that level of humor, but I was obviously thankful he had just been joking. Or, testing me.

He continued, "Her mother and I sort of expected this sooner rather than later. Her mother's request is that you let her finish school, and I stand by that as well, but we both think you will make our daughter very happy, and of course, we expect it."

I appreciated the joke, in time, but also was sure to hear the seriousness in his voice when he gave me his answer. After wiping the sweat off the receiver, I assured him it was our plan for her to finish school, and then have a wedding a few more months after that.

"I guess you expect me to pay for that too, huh?" this time letting me hear the sarcasm in his voice, figuring he had pulled me through the ringer enough.

Upon hanging up, and with one of the hardest parts over, I now had to work on doing something more romantic then just blurting out "Will you marry me?" when she walked in the door after working with horses all day.

I finally figured out how I wanted to propose. It wouldn't be for a few weeks, but still I thought it was perfect, even if the wait seemed impossible. We were planning on going to my house for an annual Cherry Blossom Festival my little town holds during the last week of April. Generally my town had a population of a few thousand. During that weekend our population grows to about 10,000. This was the weekend I decided I would propose to my wife to be.

Leading up to that trip I might as well have just put duct tape over my mouth because I hardly spoke for fear of ruining my surprise. A few times my quietness came up in conversation, but I just made an excuse about how someone at my job was bothering me and I was dwelling on that. I hated lying to my wife to be, but I knew that I would be more upset if I ruined the surprise I had in store.

After what seemed like an eternity, the day came when we would be heading to my parents house for the festival. I don't think I ever packed a car so fast, eager to get to my proposal destination. I was tempted to see how fast our little Toyota could go once we hit the highway, but not wanting to look overly eager, I tried my best to hold my composure for the five hour drive, not wanting to spoil the surprise.

After the longest drive in my life, we arrived at my

parents' house at about two in the afternoon. The festival would still be open until six o'clock, which was plenty of time to see my plan unfold, but I was still predictably nervous and anxious to get on with it. After exchanging quick pleasantries with my parents, so quick my soon-to-be fiancée said I was rude; I was ready to drag her out the door. I had told my parents I was going to propose, and assuming I called them in an hour or so and she said yes, they would have a small get together in celebration.

A few weeks before heading home I had called one of my parent's friends, Peggy, who I knew would be working a booth at the festival. The festival was entirely volunteered based, and Peggy was well known for her volunteering efforts in our town. The problem was I didn't know which booth she would be operating until I called.

"I'll be operating the goldfish booth. You know, the one where you throw ping pong balls into the bowls and win a goldfish," she told me.

I pondered for a second how I could use this in my proposal, but after a few minutes of bouncing ideas off of Peggy, I had come up with something. After getting the plans in order, I thanked her, and told her I'd see her in a few weeks.

Finally, we were heading into town to go to the festival. I was hoping I would recognize Peggy and her booth right away within the dozens and dozens of games, food trucks, and crafts that made up the event. I had no luck. Of course, my wife wanted to stop at every booth, and I impatiently dragged her from place to place. She was a bit perturbed, and I was starting to fear she would get angry and be in a bad mood during my proposal, so I tried to relax. After about an hour and a half I spotted Peggy at the goldfish booth.

When we reached the booth I told my wife to be I

wanted to try my luck. I handed Peggy a five dollar bill, which gave me 50 chances to secure a three cent fish. Peggy did a wonderful job of acting like she had never seen me before. It was showtime!

First, I had to get one of the balls into a bowl. I had played basketball in high school, so I figured this would be fairly easy. Wrong. After about 40 balls I was 0-for-40. I detected that my wife to be was getting a bit bored with the waiting, and was even questioning why I was so interested in winning a goldfish.

Growing impatient and nervous myself, I lifted the basket that was now down to about ten balls, and threw them all at once in the direction of the bowls. I watched in slow motion as one of the ping pong balls danced around the edge of a bowl before dropping in. On cue, Peggy told me congratulations and reached for a bag. My wife to be seemed relieved we would be moving on, and I had to hold her hand to keep her close by. I dropped to my knee, she didn't notice that either.

"What is that in the bag?" I asked Peggy as she handed it to me. My wife hadn't turned around yet. I tried again, this time a little louder.

"What is this in the bag?" I asked, while tugging on her hand lightly.

Finally, she turned around, and looked down at me. Inside the bag was the engagement ring, the fish swimming happily above it.

"Will you marry me?" I asked.

"Yes, yes, yes!" she replied, dropping to her knees to hug me.

I handed the bag to Peggy, who opened it and put the fish into another bag, cleaned off the ring and dried it, and handed it back to me while looking at it closely and saying, "Nice job!"

I placed the ring on her left ring finger. When I did this, the crowd I hadn't been aware of, applauded for us.

"We are going to keep the fish too, right?"

"Of course, what should we name it?" I asked.

"Bliss," she answered.

22

We decided to have the wedding in September, just five months after getting engaged. This allowed her to finish school in May, upon her parent's request, which she did, with honors. She was able to find a job just a few minutes away from my parents' house and we rented an apartment just a few miles from them.

The wedding was beautiful. Her dad did end up paying, thankfully, but on the condition we have the wedding in their hometown in North Carolina, an hour south of Hickory University. I had put up a brief argument with my wife about how I had no ties to North Carolina, but not being a very religious man, and being more concerned with just marrying her than anything else, the argument sputtered out quickly. I was getting exactly what I wanted since that first day I saw her in the campus bookstore. I would have married her on Mars if that had been her family's request.

My wife had just started her job at the local veterinary clinic so she didn't have much time for a honeymoon. Because of the small town we lived in, it was very hard for her to find relief; still, we managed to rent a very nice cabin in the Poconos Mountains. I assume the weather was lovely, but we enjoyed the inside of our cabin most of the weeklong honeymoon.

The rest of our history, despite being filled with many happy memories, is one I came to regret over my year of mourning. It wasn't that we weren't happy, it's just that after a while it seemed like every day was the same. At one point early on in our marriage we both had a desire to travel, but with her demanding job, and me picking up freelance writing jobs by the handful, we really didn't have much time to travel. Instead, we usually settled for family holidays, birthdays, and reunions for our forms of traveling. It's not that those gatherings weren't full of love and enjoyable, but I think we always wished we could experience more together.

Three years after getting married we moved into the house my parents' friends owned, the only house we would ever live in together, and the house where I still live. We had shared the idea of having children but the only other living creature that ended up living in that house, beside a stray cat or two, was Bahama.

A couple years after moving into the house, my wife went to work, despite a foot of snow on the ground, and growing. She had all but told herself she wouldn't risk it, but as the only vet in the area she felt obligated. When she finally got to work she trudged her way up the walk and to the door. As she was turning the lock she heard a whimpering from the bushes to the left of the door. When she got a closer look she saw a puppy was underneath, partially covered by the rising snow. My wife gathered up the soaked and shivering puppy and brought her inside and gave her a thorough check-up. Besides being a bit underweight, she appeared to be in good shape. I once heard that we don't pick our pets, they pick us. That was the day Bahama picked us.

We chose the name Bahama partially out of irony because we found her in a snowstorm, but also because the Bahamas was a place we had always planned to visit had we had the time or money. As it turns out, Bahama would end up doing the traveling in place of my wife, though it would take years.

The topic of children came up, but it was never the right time. For the first couple years of our marriage, I suppose that was a viable excuse. With my wife afraid she'd lose her job if she missed any considerable time, and with me picking up more jobs than ever, it was a daunting thing to think about having a baby. After a couple of more years, I think we both decided maybe having a child wasn't for us. It's not a decision I regret, but it has always held the top spot on my life's "what if" list. Especially now.

So time went on, as it does. There were weddings to go to and be in, funerals of grandparents, and the ups and downs of our personal lives. We were largely homebodies, but loved our house, generally opting to cook out on the grill and watch the sunset. The monotony of our life took a sudden turn for the worse, bringing worse news than we could have ever imagined possible. Just after our seventh year of marriage we had our yearly physicals, a chore we put little thought into.

When her blood work came back they said there was a concern, but there shouldn't be too much to worry about. We went on with our lives, I wrote, she saved animals, and tried to forget about the tests. But then there were more tests, and more tests. My wife grew more tired and stressed with each impending blood test, but still put herself into her work and never ceased making me happy regardless of all the concerns and possibilities raging in her head.

Finally, on a foggy morning in December, we heard the news that changed our lives forever.

The doctor told us it was a rare blood disease, but since they found it early they were confident they could cure it. The next year and a half was a roller coaster I have largely blocked out. During a doctor appointment my parents drug me to during my year of mourning I mentioned to the man that had been my doctor since I was a little kid, that I couldn't remember a lot of the last year and a half. He told me this was normal.

With each week my wife got more tired, and began getting headaches and having stomach issues, all symptoms of the disease. In each other's presence, and in the presence of family, we refused to call the disease by name. We didn't want to give it life. Despite our best efforts the disease continued to spread. Medicine worked, then didn't, then worked, then didn't. She missed a lot of work, and finally had to find someone to replace her, first part-time, then full-time.

We tried diets we had read about online that we were told would battle the disease, different doctors, specialty doctors, but none of them could do anything. Her prognosis was grim. First she was told she shouldn't work anymore, then it was she shouldn't leave the house, finally followed by she shouldn't leave her bed. Through it all she never complained, which at times surprisingly enough, infuriated me. Here she was dealt the worst hand in the deck but all she worried about was my well-being. She wondered how my writing was going, and if Bahama and I had encountered anything exciting on our walks. I tried to answer in an uplifting manner, but all I could do was curse God, a God I was never sure I believed in to begin with, for doing this to such a wonderful woman. The woman I loved.

When her time on earth came near an end her parents moved in, and my parents were there most of the time too. A hospice nurse brought pamphlets on what to expect as she neared death and how her family was to cope after she died. I never read them. It wasn't right. It's still not right.

For a far too short couple of weeks some combination of me and parents were in her room just talking, asking if she needed anything, asking if she wanted to see the sunlight. When we were alone she told me her fears and regrets. They were simple, really. She wished she had traveled more and she wished she would have had a child. She also wished she would have known God better. I didn't know what to say to that then, and I don't know what to say about that now. I just hope she found Him.

During the final few days Bahama refused to leave her side. Bahama had to be picked up to go outside to use the bathroom. Bahama was fairly young then and we had worried about her being off a leash, but because she was making a beeline right back to her side, there was no need for one. Her father had read to me in one of the pamphlets that often people die when they are alone, even if there were 10 people in the room as recently as a minute ago. That's the route my wife decided to take to the great unknown.

There was one exception: Bahama never left her side. On her final night, I walked into her room to see her breathing shallow and labored, but she still greeted me with a smile despite not opening her eyes much, if at all. In what was my closest supernatural experience I've ever had, I saw the door of the room narrow as I walked out of it for the final time in her life. I had the overwhelming feeling that when I walked through the door I would never see her alive again. Shortly after I kissed her goodbye, I had walked outside and onto the deck. A few minutes later her father came out and put his arm around me and buried his head in my shoulder and began crying. He didn't have to say a word. A few seconds later, Bahama joined us on the deck.

23

For a ride that amounts to almost 3,000 miles, I was largely fixated on thinking about my wife during my trip west. There were no major traffic or weather delays, and Bahama enjoyed the trip just fine, swapping time between sticking her nose out of the back window and sitting in the passenger side seat. She was blessed with a strong bladder, so she doesn't need to make a lot of stops. It's usually me making those stops.

Despite getting a rise in excitement level when I saw the lights, I was way too exhausted to do any exploring that first night. My final day of driving started in Tucumcari, New Mexico and ended just off the Las Vegas strip – about 12 hours of driving. The town of Tucumcari had seen better days, but there was a unique aspect about it. The historic Route 66 has been virtually wiped away as it was known 50 years ago in most parts of the country, but in Tucumcari it looks close to what it used to be back then. It has modern touches of today, with McDonald's and other chain restaurants and stores appearing, but many of the hotels and diners have been there since Route 66's heyday.

When I called home and told my parents of my whereabouts, which I had been doing every week or so during my adventure, I told my dad about my travels through this town, which brought up good memories for him. My father's father was a traveling salesman, usually driving up and down the east coast, but once a year he had to drive out to California for a big meeting with all the bosses of the company. This meeting took place during the summer, so my dad would drive along with him, where they used Route 66 exclusively.

I found a little pharmacy and gift shop before I headed out of Tucumcari and picked up five "historic" postcards to send back home to him. He also remembered driving through Vegas during his school years but never dreamed of asking his dad to stop as his father was a deeply religious man who never would have dreamt of putting money down on a game of chance. For the most part, my father followed those same values, though he does buy a lottery ticket every now and then when the prize gets really high.

I was then in the city where everyone was hoping to cash a lottery ticket, whether it was with roulette, blackjack, Keno, or poker. Growing up with a father like I did, I didn't know if this was the right city for me, but like I mentioned back in Key West, I was there because I was looking for the exact opposite type of place. I would soon be getting what I asked for.

Even at 32 years old, I wondered what my father would think of me spending a considerable amount of time in a city his dad wouldn't even mention by name, especially by its nickname. So, naturally I didn't bring it up when I spoke to him, though he did ask about it from time to time.

That first night I booked a room at a resort and casino called South Point. Technically it was on the Las Vegas Strip, but it was still a few miles away from the main casinos everyone recognizes on commercials and television. For the first night that would have to do because they accepted dogs and I was too tired to go any farther. After checking in, and having a few very nice drunk women celebrating a bachelorette party pet Bahama on the way to my room, I dropped her off and went down to the casino to look around for a bite to eat.

What I remember most about that night is, number one starving, and number two wondering exactly what I was doing there. As usual with me during this trip I worried about my stomach first. Figuring out why I was there could wait until later.

I sat in a 50's style restaurant near the back of the giant casino floor called Steak 'n Shake. All I know is that they had an amazing double steak burger with cheese and above average fries, and the best chocolate shake I have ever had. I seriously considered ordering seconds, on everything, but I didn't want to pay for it in the morning, my first full day in Las Vegas. Still, I was stuffed and waddled back into my room. I had once read that people find it hard to sleep in Vegas, but after a 12 hour drive, and a belly full of grease and sugar, I didn't have that problem.

The next morning I called around for hotels that accepted pets but weren't as expensive as South Point. I figured that because South Point was one of the farthest casinos away from the main popular casinos that I wouldn't have luck finding one cheap enough to house Bahama and I for the duration of our trip. I was right, I didn't have any luck, but after talking to a chatty receptionist at one of the dozen hotels I called, she suggested that I try to find a furnished place. She told me that almost no casinos in the heart of the city would accept a dog and that I could find a place off the strip for a fraction of the price it would cost for me to stay at a casino for any significant amount of time.

While I didn't have an idea of where to start, I had read that Henderson, the next city over from Vegas and only about 15 minutes away from the strip, was nice. I figured my best bet, one of the few bets I actually made in Vegas, would be to try apartment and condo complexes, though I had no idea if they would offer furnished, short-term, options. Still, I had to start somewhere.

After getting to Henderson, most of my conversations with complex employees started and ended with one of two questions. Number one was always "Do you accept dogs?" and if that was a yes we were always shut down with "Do you have furnished places?"

After a long day of inquiring at seven or eight different apartment and townhome complexes I resigned myself to the fact that I would have to probably take to the internet to find a place, but not knowing the area, and having to wait for people to have time to show me their rental unit could take another week, at least. Just as I was getting ready to go back to South Point I spotted a set of buildings just off the exit that were "corporate apartments." I have never had been a part of any corporation, but I figured if I had the money they would let me stay – and my little dog too.

I was right. After working out a pay schedule, including a little money down, I decided I would stay there. I chose a 750 square foot apartment, with washer/dryer, full kitchen, slightly old furniture and an older television. But the property included a small dog run in the back, which was its main selling point. This would more than do, I remember thinking.

The rest of the day I got settled, stocked the fridge with fruits and vegetables, something foreign to me on this trip so far, and relaxed. Two nights in Vegas and I haven't been on The Strip yet. I felt I was doing it wrong, though I didn't know exactly what it was I should be doing.

The next morning I got up with the intention of

going straight to The Strip. I let Bahama know that'd I'd be back later. A pro at this game by now, she curled up on the bed as I gathered up my wallet and keys. She was asleep by the time I walked out. Up on the 5th floor and windows that didn't open, there was little concern for unwanted cats visiting us there.

It was 9 a.m. on a Thursday in early October when I hit the Vegas Strip for the first time. It was already busier than what I would expect this early. People posed for pictures in every direction you could see, including up on the pedestrian walkways that went between casinos and over the busy road. I got onto The Strip near the Stratosphere, which is generally considered the beginning of The Strip. As I drove towards the middle of The Strip, the buildings got more impressive. One thing I learned very early about Vegas is that if you placed a Casino like The Sahara in any other city in America, it would be considered one of the nicest hotels in the country. In Las Vegas, there were about ten hotels that were considered nicer within two miles.

My first stop on the Vegas Strip, not including traffic, came at the Bellagio. I choose the Bellagio because I instantly recognized the fountains from TV and movies. Now I was doing something "Vegasy." Every half an hour they shoot the fountains into the air, while accompanied by some famous piece of classical music. You can choose to watch the show from The Strip sidewalk or you can walk towards the entrance of the Bellagio and find a place to watch it anywhere on the circle that makes a full loop from the sidewalk to the front door. The prime position predictably is center on The Strip sidewalk. I parked my car using the valet, asking the ultimate tourist question – How much does valet cost? - Only to be told it was free everywhere on The Strip, and pretty much free everywhere in Vegas.

Unlike a side view mirror in a car, objects are farther than they appear in Vegas, not closer. On the half hour mark I had only made it about halfway through the circle, so I watched the show uninterrupted, but from a bad view. I had to wait another half-hour before I saw the show from straight on, but just coming from Key West where a few people walking in front of you was considered a traffic jam, the congestion of people was too much. I started walking back into the casino before the show was over. Some tourist I was.

I walked in to the Bellagio and was blown away by the sheer size of the place. The lobby itself was a prime picture taking spot for tourists. After navigating my way through that maze, I walked onto the casino floor. Right away I could tell the building blew South Point away aesthetically. Plus, the people were dressed in a much nicer fashion, in a way that suggested they just wanted to be seen. I was wearing a New River University shirt and khaki shorts. I stuck out like a sore thumb.

After walking around for a few minutes I encountered a problem I would have my entire stay in Vegas – dry mouth. Surprisingly enough it turns out the desert is dry, and it has no issue sucking the moisture in my body out like a vacuum storage bag. I picked up a four dollar bottle of water at the food court, and began to make my retreat for the exit. I considered leaving my car at valet and walking up Las Vegas Boulevard, but after taking over an hour to walk a circle on the Bellagio's property I opted to get my car. It also didn't help that I had gained a few pounds since the start of my trip. Between my new found gut and dry mouth I couldn't completely convince myself I could make it back to the Bellagio later.

While I was waiting for my car I saw others giving the valets a dollar or two upon receiving their car. I had a stray dollar in my pocket, so I looked a little less like a tourist on my way out then on the way in. I doubted I was fooling anyone, but the Valet asked me if I needed directions.

"Yeah, where's the famous 'Welcome to Las Vegas' sign that you see in the movies?" I had remembered movies where you saw characters drive by it somewhere way out in the desert, so I didn't know if I was going to see it that day, but wanted to know anyway.

"Sure bud, it's about a mile up the road when you turn right out of here. It's in the median, you can't miss it."

"But I thought it was way out in the desert? Is this a different one?"

"Oh no, they moved it into the city years ago so the cops could keep a better eye on it. People were vandalizing it almost every day. It was costing the city thousands to keep repairing it."

I thanked him, handed him the dollar, and headed for the sign. Sure enough, it was right in the median with a parking lot so people could get in and out on both sides of the road. It was there that I first saw the epitome of Las Vegas, an Elvis impersonator joining a newly married couple posing for pictures. It turns out the Elvis impersonator also married them.

It was doing things like this on my trip that always made me feel the oddest. I was already concerned about being in Las Vegas because I was afraid I was being seen as the "creepy old guy." In Vegas, with so many beautiful young people running around, it was very easy to feel like that.

Taking pictures of a "Welcome to Las Vegas"

sign, and asking a young couple to take a picture of me under it, didn't help. It was here that I also began thinking about my wife and how fun it would have been to do something like that with her. I remember thinking that my mind didn't automatically go to being depressed, which was new to me when thinking of things I missed out on with my wife. But it did upset me enough that it took some starch out of me. After getting my picture and taking a picture for a few other groups of tourists, I went back to the car. This time I took the highway, deciding I had had enough of The Strip for one day.

24

I had read that one of the hardest things to do while visiting Las Vegas was keeping up with a normal routine. It was really easy to get lost in gambling and partying and drinking. Before you know it, you haven't eaten a proper meal or showered in three days. For me, I thought I would be able to avoid many of these pitfalls because of flying solo on this trip, and Bahama.

I decided to call my sister and check in before heading out the next morning for another day of exploring in Vegas. My sister had some pretty surprising news. After having to be talked in to getting Pinky, she had now been talked into a second dog. My little niece was turning into quite the negotiator without her uncle around. Cassidy's argument was that her new puppy needed another new puppy to play with. My sister made sure to thank me for that with her own colorful choice of words.

When I told Chloe I was in Vegas, she got excited. She had visited there quite a few times with her husband when they were together. She told me about her favorite things to do, including her favorite restaurants. I jotted these down, but was listening most when she mentioned food. She told me the buffets are out of this world, and that most of them have the biggest plates she's ever seen, wider than a steering wheel. She also told me that it seems every casino on the strip has a good cheeseburger, but one of them stood out more than the other. Chloe told me I had to go to the Burger Bar at Mandalay Bay. I should also choose this place because I can sit at the bar and maybe meet a few people, as it was apparently common in Vegas for people visiting alone to sit at the bars. I was already worried about being the "creepy old guy," so I wasn't sure how I felt about sitting alone at a bar, but the prospect of a tasty burger outweighed most of those concerns.

At least at the bar I could almost pretend I was sitting with someone because I hated thinking I was being stared at when I was eating alone in restaurants. I loved burgers, so I decided I would waste no time in visiting her recommendation and determined I would go that same day. After a quick jaunt with Bahama in the dog run, I headed to the Mandalay Bay.

Mandalay Bay was just a touch below the level of Bellagio, but it was still a very nice and clean atmosphere. Comparing the two places wasn't heavily on my mind though because I was hungry and didn't care about ambiance at that moment. I headed up an escalator to the Mandalay Place Shops, which amounted to a mall that also acted as a walkway between the Mandalay Bay and the Luxor, one of the more iconic sights on the Strip with its giant beam of light coming out of the tip of the pyramid structure. I found the restaurant easy enough. Seeing I was alone, I assumed, the hostess asked if I wanted to sit at the bar. I nodded, and she led the way.

The bar of the Burger Bar was located to the left side of the narrow restaurant. With the majority of the patrons sitting behind you when you sat down at the bar, and the rest sitting next to you, it was hard to do any serious people watching. People watching in most other cities in the world may just be a way to pass the time, but here in Vegas, it was literally one of the top 10 things to do. Seriously, I read it on a website. When you are in Vegas alone it ranks closer to the top of that list. Unfortunately for me I could see only a couple people in the restaurant from my vantage point. But fortunately for me, the ones that were in my view were women and attractive.

The uniform of choice for the employees at the Burger Bar was a tight corset that left a viewing window for most of the stomach, and a cut that left offered another window for a decent portion of the chest. Amazingly enough, at the particular moment, I didn't give the outfit a second thought, as I had worked up quite the appetite.

"What can I get you?" A female bartender asked me as I looked up from the menu.

"Fat Tire, please." I watched her walk over to a corner and grab a bottle. I forgot to mention their black pants were also tight. I looked away as she came back. I've never been the smoothest guy.

"Are you ready to order, or do you need another minute?" she asked.

"Just another minute or so, thanks," I replied. Truth is I hadn't had much time to look at the menu, instead focusing on her.

I don't know when I didn't feel guilty looking at or thinking of another woman since my wife died. For a long time, I felt that I was disrespecting her even though she told me she fully expected me to get married again. She would always add as a joke, that always had a ring of seriousness to it, that I need a woman to take care of me. When she said that, it made me wince, because I didn't want there to be anyone else but her taking care of me, but as the months turned into a year, and now almost two, I realized she was probably right. A woman had always taken care of me – from my wife, to my mother, to Jean for the last month, or so. For my entire life there had been very few moments when I didn't have a woman to thank for my mere existence.

When the attractive waitress returned, and I had

found enough time to stop leering at her, I ordered the Kobe beef burger and a combination of three different types of fries with various sauces. The burger, the most expensive I had ever bought in my life, came in at around twenty bucks, but it was worth every penny. My sister had picked a winner. I remember wondering between bites what other food gems I had missed out on by not talking to my sister. My gut appreciated us making up for lost time.

Between bites of burger, I talked with the bartender who took my order, Jen. Jen didn't look exactly like her co-workers, or many of the other ladies that make up the service industry in Las Vegas. Don't get me wrong, she was very attractive, and it wasn't just because of the corset and tight pants. She had long lean limbs indicating that she was no stranger to the gym. Her smile was genuine and warm. She wore light make-up, not nearly as much as her co-workers. Her hair was cut shorter than most women, but not short enough to be considered a "boy cut." Her short hair made her warm facial features stand out. As I drank more Fat Tires, they began to stand out even more.

She looked different than most of her co-workers because she seemed a bit older, but again, I don't mean that in a negative way. She had an air of confidence that was not manufactured. She was very comfortable with herself.

I wasn't sure this was what my sister meant when she said I would find company sitting at a bar in Vegas, but I was more than happy to be talking to Jen between bites and not the burly man on the stool next to me. My luck of late, as documented, hadn't been great with ladies, but at least at this moment my trusty sidekick Bahama had no chance of jumping after manatees. Still, I kept the conversation superficial, and what I considered safe. I told her I was a traveling writer, and about my time in the Keys. She seemed equally superficial in her answers, rightfully so, perhaps not completely trusting the guy in Vegas by himself, but also said she was a bit of a world traveler.

As I continued drinking I began fearing that it was only a matter of time before I did something stupid, like fall off my stool, or spit a french fry in her direction. I began planning my retreat. This was the most normal conversation I had had with a woman in over two years and I wanted to be able to have something to draw back on whenever I decided I was ready to play the field again, if ever. Despite my warning to myself to leave before embarrassing myself I didn't stop talking with Jen until just a few minutes before The Burger Bar was ready to close. Yet another reason I had to thank my sister for recommending this place.

Jen handed me my bill, and I could see that about half of the 6 or 8 beers I had consumed had been comped by her. My first comped drink in Vegas! I had arrived. Best part was it hadn't cost me a cent in gambling losses. I thanked her probably one too many times, before leaving a tip big enough that would have been plenty to pay for those 6 to 8 beers. I remembered when she handed me back the receipt she looked at me almost expectantly, but I figured I must have had some dipping sauce residue on my lip or something. Before I could risk embarrassing myself anymore, I stuffed the receipt in my pocket, thanked her for the 34th time, and headed out.

For the first time since I had been in Vegas I gambled, attributing that decision to the buzz I was feeling and because I wanted to sober up before driving home. I considered a cab, but I thought that the cab fare would be astronomical from here to my place in Henderson. Plus, for the life of me, I couldn't figure out the address of where I was staying, and had no desire of explaining step by step directions to the cabdriver through the slurred speech I had acquired over the last few hours. While sitting at a 25 cent blackjack machine, sobering up, I remembered a story from my 21st birthday.

I had gone home for the weekend solo, my wife, who was my girlfriend at the time, having to stay behind to do some field work with a horse or something. My best friend from high school, Ryan, was also home that weekend. Ryan and I drifted apart during college because he went to school in New York, and after this particular story I can't remember us ever hanging out ever again. Our little city was always too small for Ryan and everyone who knew him felt the same. Last I heard, he was working in an office in a skyscraper in NYC as an investment banker. Regardless, our friendship went out with a bang.

Ryan decided he was going to drive me over the state-line to West Virginia so we can go to a strip-club, where they were legal. He told me not to tell my wife-to-be – I did anyway, she was fine with it believing "boys will be boys" – and we hit the road for the two hour drive.

Telling the talent at a strip club that it's your birthday can go one of two ways. It can be amazing if you like the attention. Or, it can be a horrible experience, for the same reason. It was quite a different experience from having the staff at Applebee's sing "Happy Birthday" to you, which is how I spent my 20th birthday.

I experienced both of those feelings – amazing and awkwardness – over the course of the night. As these things go, the drinks flowed and the humiliation ceased to matter anymore. I have slight, foggy memories of our trip to West Virginia, but I couldn't tell if those memories came from Ryan rehashing them for me, or me actually remembering them.

I had been on the stage, and at one point had three of Sandy's employees on me and wrapped around me in some fashion. I also went back to the private room, but was so out of it at this point that the lady felt bad for me and returned me to my friend. Also, I didn't have my wallet on me deeming me pointless to the woman.

I didn't have my wallet on me because earlier in the night when one of the girls was dancing for me I had presented her with my entire wallet because I was having a problem taking a dollar bill out of it. Ryan says the lady thought this was a joke and sort of just smiled, but didn't return the wallet right away. Ryan high tailed it across the room, from the bar to the stage, to retrieve it for me. In short, if Jen would have kept feeding me Fat Tires she could have had a huge tip, including credit cards.

After playing Blackjack until I felt sober enough to drive back to the apartment, leaving a big 75 cent winner, I walked out to the valet. On the drive home I wondered how many other people in this town have had the "how drunk am I?" talk to themselves before getting behind the wheel. I made a plea to myself that I wouldn't do that anymore if I got home safely. I did.

I took Bahama outside to the dog run, with the plan to let her stretch her legs for a few minutes. Thankfully Bahama seemed sympathetic of my plight, walking back over to me after doing her business, ready to go upstairs. When we got back to my room I emptied my pockets, put their contents on the dresser, and crashed into bed. It wasn't until the next morning I realized there had been a reason for Jen's longing look before I left the Burger Bar.

25

I woke up the next morning feeling more than a bit hung over. After a hot shower and a complimentary continental breakfast I was beginning to feel a bit more human. I took Bahama out to the run, owing her from last night. This time Bahama stayed longer because a business executive looking type was out with his dog. While he was on the phone, Bahama and his mutt wore themselves out before both tapping out and heading back to the leg of their respective owners.

Back in the room I wanted to make sure I had remembered my wallet and credit card from the night before, now that my mind belonged to me a little more than it did last night. I went to the dresser where I had unceremoniously dumped the contents of my pockets. I spotted loose change, wallet, and phone, and grabbed a receipt to throw it into the trashcan. Just as I was getting ready to ball it up it, some writing on the receipt caught my attention and I thought I had spent more than I originally comprehended. When I looked at the receipt I realized my bill wouldn't have amounted to 10 numbers, no matter how many beers I had. It was Jen's phone number. On a receipt.

Only once in my life had I been impacted so much by a phone number on a receipt, and I married the owner of that number. I stumbled back a few steps and sat on the bed and stared at the number. And stared. And stared.

A million thoughts went through my head, all of them revolving around my wife. I knew that eventually in my life I would pursue another woman, but in no way was I prepared for it to come in the same form as the girl I had wished to spend the rest of my life with. I mentioned that my wife had told me it was okay with her to pursue other relationships once she passed, but I didn't expect it to be so soon. *Soon?* I questioned myself. It had been nearly two years. But with me just now coming out of my shell it seemed like much, much sooner.

To say that I wasn't lonely over that time period would be a lie. For many months I associated loneliness with just my wife. Over time that thought of loneliness became a broader feeling, one not just associated with my wife. I knew the day would come that I would have a chance to not be lonely, but again, I didn't expect it too soon.

There was also a very good chance that I was overanalyzing things with Jen. Just because one girl gave you a phone number on a receipt didn't mean you were going to marry her. Sure, I was already 1 for 1 at that point, but Jen giving me her number that way was purely coincidental, right? If you are the type to believe in signs, and I never fully embraced the idea personally of believing in signs, then this was one as clear as it would get. During my darkest days I had asked for a sign, but now that I was coming out of my funk it seemed I had received a pretty easy one to interpret.

Perhaps Jen was just looking for a fling. We were in Las Vegas. She knew from our conversation, when I told her I was a traveling writer, that I probably wouldn't be around for long, and maybe after my third or fourth beer I was giving off the impression that I wouldn't mind a fling, though that certainly wasn't my intention. At the very least, it was a chance for me to potentially have a real conversation with a woman, even if the actual relationship amounted to nothing.

After staring at the receipt for longer than I had ever stared at any other receipt in my life, with the exception of one, I put it into my pocket and sat down in front of the computer, knowing I wouldn't get much work done that day, but would pretend to try. The taking out of the receipt and putting it back into my pocket was an occurrence that happened another 100 times, give or take, over the next three days, so much so I had to cut back on that habit for fear I would smear the ink or rip the receipt and not be able to read it.

At some point over those few days I knew I was going to call her, but still held back. It wasn't enough for me to just say I'll call her and see what happens from there. No, I went through every possible scenario imaginable. I wondered if she gave her phone number to every lonely guy that sat at her bar. I also wondered, this being the city of working class girls, if that when I called I would be directed to her pimp. This was silly, but this is what you do when you haven't made a phone call to a woman with relationship potential in over a decade.

On the third day I decided I was going to call. After all that thinking, my game plan going into the conversation was to not think. Say "hello," and go from there. I called.

She answered on the second ring.

"Hello," she answered hesitantly, most likely because she didn't recognize my number.

"Hey, this is Mike from…,"

"Oh, hey, I was wondering if you were going to call me. How do you like Vegas so far?"

"Um, ahhh, I like it, I haven't done much more than eat," I followed that with nervous laughter.

"Maybe you should change that. What are you

doing tonight? I get off at 11, I can show you around some if you'd like."

"I would like that, should I meet you at your work or..."

"Yeah, that will be fine, see ya then," she said. I could picture her smile from a few nights before, in turn, making me smile.

"Ok, see ya then."

I'm glad I had eaten breakfast already. No way was I eating again until after our date tonight, I thought.

Our date. Wow.

26

I waited patiently and comfortably with Bahama until it was time to go. Yeah, right. I was a wreck. Going through all the potential outcomes of our phone call had be stressful enough. Going through all the situations of what could happen when I was physically with Jen was a different ball game.

Every hour progressed the same way. I would work myself up, and then calm myself down. I told myself all I was doing was just meeting another person, a fellow being from the human race. Even if it turned out to be a horrible experience it wasn't like I hadn't been through worse. That line of thinking helped for about ten minutes.

I tried to write, but wrote just a few sentences. I was stuck in some universe I could never hope to comprehend. When it was finally time for me to go, I was both in a full sweat, but thankful it was at least time to move. I left early, a specialty of mine, to guarantee I would get there in time. After leaving the car with the valet I still had 45 minutes before I had to meet Jen.

That was great. That left me plenty of time to go to the bathroom four more times, and wipe my hands on my pants thirty times to ensure that my handshake didn't bathe hers. With about 15 minutes to go I found Burger Bar, as if I had forgotten to get there. Not wanting to seem over anxious, I walked around the shops and timed my entrance to be right at the front door of the Burger Bar at exactly 11, casually as I possibly could.

I didn't see her right away, and my mind went right to thinking she probably stood me up. I envisioned her hot friends calling her up and telling her they were going to do something better than have her hang out with some loser she had met at her bar. Near the end of that ridiculous idea, she walked out.

In all my thoughts leading up to that minute, I had envisioned her going on our date with her tight pants and corset. Instead she had on a pair of jeans and a blue sleeveless shirt, cut low.

"Hi there," she said, and came in for a hug. I was only previously worried about my hand sweating during a handshake. Now I had to hope my 14 layers of deodorant did their job, as I was unprepared for such a physical gesture this early in our date.

"Hey, what do you have in store for me tonight?" I hoped this sounded platonic, but if you think about it you can make a sexual innuendo about just about anything.

"If you like rides, I thought maybe we could go to the Stratosphere and try out some of their rides. I have been here eight months and I have never done them yet," she said with the smile I had thought about many times over the last few days.

I gulped once, stronger than I anticipated, and said, "Yeah, that sounds fun."

I hadn't been to the Stratosphere yet, but any tourist can see from looking up at the needle shaped structure that the rides hang precariously off the side of the building. From the ground the rides look like they are 10,000 miles in the air. That's just another desert mirage, it's really only closer to 1,000 feet. Hearing that information from Jen didn't do much to calm my stomach. Yet another reason I was glad I hadn't eaten much today.

We decided to take a cab over to the Stratosphere. I had hoped to use this time for getting to know her better, but unfortunately we had a very talkative cab driver. I think Sal thought we were longtime girlfriend and boyfriend because he kept bringing up all the chapels around town where we could get married.

"Hell, we could do a drive-thru and you won't have to get out of the car," he added with a New York accent. He'd be our witness. How nice of him. I had heard taxi drivers try to get you to strip clubs because they get paid by these establishments by bringing in customers. I had never heard of one getting paid for getting people to get married. The economy had been down, so who knows?

The Stratosphere wasn't as sparkly as some of the other casinos, but it had plenty of customers that night. Jen told me that they have a loyal customer base because it's the closest casino to a lot of the surrounding neighborhoods. Also, many tourists like it for the reason we were there: the views of the Strip and the rides on the top of the needle.

I was nervous to be going on these rides, but I was also nervous because I was about to go on these rides with someone I had just met. Should I scream? Should I wear a poker face? What will she do? Will she grab onto me if she gets scared?

We walked through the casino and stopped at the ticket booth. I paid 50 bucks for the two of us for a ride up the elevator to the top and unlimited access to the rides.

We entered the elevator with about 15 other folks. One of them asked the elevator operator "how's it going?" He replied, "up and down." Ah, elevator humor.

When we reached the top I was awestruck by the view. The huge circular windows showed the best view in the city of the entire Las Vegas Strip

"What brought you out to Vegas? Are you from here?" was all I could come up with for my opening line. Smooth.

"I don't know what exactly brought me out here," she said. I can relate, I thought.

"What do you mean? Just traveling?"

"It's complicated, but at the same time it's not. Three years ago I had a pretty tough break-up that got kind of nasty when we finally broke up for good. At the time I felt like my life was shattered – he was my high school sweetheart – but after thinking long and hard about what he put me through I realized it was for the better," she added a nervous laughter at the end.

"I'm traveling too; I just came from Florida," forgetting I had told her that a few nights ago. Again, smooth.

"Oh yeah, you started telling me about that at the bar. The Keys, right?"

"Yup, that's right, sorry I forgot I told you this. I was in Key West."

"Lucky dog! I've always wanted to go there."

With that, we had walked outside and found ourselves standing in front of our first ride of the night, X-Scream. X-Scream didn't look all that intimidating. That is, if it had been on the ground. At 900 feet in the air and the fact it thrust you 50 feet away from the building into the open air changed my feelings. I made a joke about the "X" in X-Scream being reserved for the cuss word you yell before screaming on the ride. Not my best work, but it received a polite chuckle in response.

The ride was a half teeter-totter, half roller coaster contraption. Jen and I, and about 15 other passengers, hopped on. Luckily we were sitting in the back so I wouldn't get a direct look at the ground. This also improved my chances of not crying like a baby in front of my date.

We got in and the ride operator made sure we were secure. I checked three more times just to confirm. The actual ride doesn't move much. You are on a short track, but your cart shoots over the edge, then straight down. It was certainly the most my heart rate had raised in a few months, which probably wasn't a bad thing. The ride was great, but what I was left pondering was if Jen's hand and sizable nails digging into my thigh were a result of her trying to make contact with me, or just holding on for dear life.

Without having a chance to catch our breath we walked over to the other side of the Stratosphere observation deck and jumped on Insanity. While I hadn't seen it in action, it was pretty clear what it was going to do. When the ride started a mechanical arm reached farther and farther out until there was only air between our shoes and the Las Vegas land. Then, we spun. Once again I was glad I hadn't eaten anything, though on this ride I briefly considered I could faint from fear. Luckily each rider was in their own separate compartment on this ride so I was free to close my eyes and imagine myself in a fetal position until we were back on solid ground. The first few steps off the ride were shaky, at best, but it was a much shorter fall if I tripped here than if I would have fallen off Insanity.

I already knew we were heading for another ride, Big Shot. Big Shot operated on the needle of the Stratosphere. Of all the rides I thought this one seemed the sanest. You sit in a circle with the other passengers, facing the open air.

I was wrong. I was in mid-sentence when the Big Shot took off for the top of the needle. I spent most of the remaining part of the night trying to get my breath and hoping my stomach would remove itself from my throat. After shooting up a couple of hundred feet at a couple of hundred miles an hour we stopped. I didn't remember much from high school anymore, but I remembered what Newton taught me. What goes up must come down. My brief hope that we would be allowed off the ride at the top lasted just that long – briefly. We shot back down at another couple hundred miles of hour. Again, I was thankful that nobody could see you on this ride, so you were left with your own fears, and tears, should they come.

When we returned safely to the ground I suggested to Jen maybe we can get a drink before she suggested seconds on any of the previous rides.

"Yeah, we can get hammered and then go do the rides all over again!" she said, striking fear in me.

"Um…yeah…we…"

"I'm just kidding!" she said, adding a punch to my arm for emphasis.

"Whew."

27

We considered getting drinks at the Top of the World bar, but the music was so loud we changed our minds. I thought of this as a good thing – that she wanted to move locations – because we had hardly had a chance to talk yet. We went back downstairs, and after making a round and seeing the other three or four bars were just as loud and busy, we decided on a quieter looking restaurant. It wasn't exactly the hippest place in Vegas, but at least we wouldn't have to scream at each other.

When we sat down in our booth there was a moment of quiet that I was afraid would remain. Maybe I had been lucky we hadn't had a chance to talk because maybe we would have just sat there and stared at each other until we found our chance to retreat. I spoke first.

"How'd you like those rides? You said it was the first time you'd been on those?"

"Yup, first time. I loved it. I hadn't been on a roller coaster since I was a little girl."

"Me too, well, since I was a little boy, not a little girl.", I had been on a few roller coasters as an adult, but that was more to make a joke then purposely lying about something so trivial. Leaving me no chance to continue my odd approach at conversation, she took over.

"So, you mentioned last night you aren't married? Have you ever been?"

The question was innocent and to be expected, but caught me off guard. Perhaps if I hadn't been caught off guard I would have continued with my lying, but instead I answered honestly, in full detail.

"I was married for just over nine years, but my wife died about a year and a half ago from cancer." I wanted to look deep into my bottle of beer, but looked up.

"Awww, I'm so sorry, I can't imagine," she said. It was the first time I had seen Jen have anything other than a smile, or hint of a smile, on her face.

"Thank you." Before she could say anything else, I asked her if she had been married before.

"No, I was in a serious relationship, but it turned bad really quickly," she said, adding that nervous laughter again. "I had lived in Kansas City my entire life, and for many years was perfectly content with the idea of growing old there with Sam, my ex. After we broke up, I got in the car and just started driving."

"That sounds familiar," I said.

"What do you mean?"

"No, please, I'm sorry for interrupting."

She spent a few months in and around San Diego driving up and down the Pacific Coast Highway, stopping for a week or two at a time at many of the different beach towns. When she was ready to move on from there she headed north, all the way to Seattle. In Seattle she got an apartment and enjoyed walking around downtown, ducking in and out of bars and restaurants whenever it began to rain. She liked Seattle, so she decided to stay almost half a year. She laughed when she told me how clichéd her job was while she was there. She worked at a coffee shop. I laughed and said, "When in Rome."

She eventually tired of the rain, and the winter had been colder than she had expected, so she traveled to a place where rain and cold weather are rarely an issue – Las Vegas. She told me that despite being a homebody for most of her life she had always enjoyed meeting people and she knew she would get a chance to do that in Vegas. She hadn't expected on getting the job as a bartender at Burger Bar, as her only experience with making drinks came at the café in Seattle. I bit my tongue, as I could think of two very good reasons she got the job – her personality and her looks were both worthy of a job in Las Vegas. For some reason I didn't think her background making lattes in Seattle had factored too much in the hiring process. She'd been working there eight months now, the transition from coffee to alcohol being easier than she anticipated.

I asked her if she had always worked in the service industry, but she said no. In Kansas City, she had been of all things, an accountant. I had to bite my tongue yet again to not tell her she had to be far and away the hottest accountant in history. She told me as a child she grew up with a love of numbers and enjoyed math so much she asked her teachers for extra work. She didn't want to seem like a teacher's pet to her friends, so she would sneak back in after they had been dismissed for the day. She began doing her parents' bills when she was just 12 years old, finding ways to save her family – parents and a younger brother – a lot of money. She went to school in Manhattan, Kansas, about four hours from her home, the farthest away she had ever been from home.

"I'm so sorry, I've talked so much! You must think I'm a blabber mouth," she said. I hadn't thought that at all.

"That's perfectly fine," I said.

"Listen, I hope you don't think that I don't want to hear about you, but I am exhausted from being on my feet all day. I won't keep you in suspense and make you wonder if I want to go out with you again. I want to do this again. Soon."

I was sad the night was ending, but it was already very late, or very early, depending on how you look at it. Also, I wasn't sure I was ready to divulge as much information as she had to me. I was going to need some time to digest the last few hours. I was already looking forward to our next date and opening up to her like she had done for me.

Jen took a taxi from the Stratosphere, telling me her place was actually closer there than if we went back and got my car. Just as our date ended and before hopping in the cab, she came in for the hug. This time I was ready for it.

I offered to pay her taxi, but she said, "You don't have to do that, but with the tip you gave me the other night you sort of are." I watched her get in the taxi and flash that smile I was beginning to like so much, one last time before she faded away into the Vegas night.

28

I spent the next couple of days writing in the room, reinvigorated, and hanging out with Bahama. Bahama hadn't been on a ride for a while, so I decided to drive her around town. For the first time in my life, and hers too, we went into a dog bakery. If you were blindfolded and placed into the middle of this dog bakery you wouldn't have thought twice before eating a piece of dessert if offered to you. The Canine Cannoli, Boxer Biscotti, and Beagle Beignets all looked like their human edible counterparts.

While I was told they looked like the real thing, I was also told they didn't taste like the real thing. Good to know. Though there was nothing in there that would be considered unsafe for a human to consume. Bahama didn't care who or what it was intended for, as she scarfed down one of almost everything. After taking a couple more for the road, we headed to a nearby dog park one of the cashiers at the dog bakery had recommended.

When we got to the park, there were a handful of other dogs. I was slightly hesitant, because most of them were bigger than Bahama, but at the end I figured she'd be fine. When we first got there she stayed mostly by my side, occasionally going off to meet another dog or two, only to come back.

The owner of one of the bigger dogs, a man in his 50's, brought out a brightly colored Frisbee that caught the attention of Bahama. Almost seeking approval from me, Bahama looked up at me as to ask, "Can I play?" I nodded, and she was off.

There were a few benches off to the side of the gated dog park, and I parked myself on one. After sitting for a few minutes, occasionally petting a wandering dog, my phone rang. It was Jen. I answered.

"Hey Mike, how are you?" she asked, her smile radiating through the phone.

"I'm good, and you?"

"I'm good, listen, it turns out that I have a couple of days off unexpectedly because they are training a new girl and I haven't been there long enough to do that. I was hoping we can hang out tonight if you aren't busy? I won't bail on you like I did a few nights ago."

"Oh, no worries about that at all. That sounds great. Where should I pick you up?"

"I can come to you. I want to meet Bahama, too!"

I gave her the address to my apartment, the same address I had forgotten a few nights ago when considering a cab when leaving Burger Bar, with the plan of meeting her in a couple of hours. Just as I was pondering the thought of having a girl in my apartment for the first time in what seemed like forever, I heard a loud cry. When I looked up, Bahama was in the middle of a tumble that lasted about ten yards. When she came to a stop she was holding her right front paw off the ground.

"What happened?!" I asked the man who was throwing the Frisbee without trying to sound too panicked.

"My dog Bruce there somehow got under your dog and when he jumped up for the Frisbee he lifted yours into the air! I'm so sorry; Bruce would never do anything to intentionally hurt anything."

I looked at Bruce, a big burly looking retriever. He had obvious concern for his new friend Bahama, as he was looking between her and his master.

"It's okay, these things happen. You know a good

vet around here?"

"Yes, Bruce's vet is up on Sahara, not far from here, I could go with you and make sure you get in right away to see the doc."

"No that's all right…well, could you call and tell them we're on our way?"

"Sure thing; I'm so sorry, if you need my information let me know. Here's my number."

I scooped up Bahama, who hadn't moved much, other than a few steps only to end up with her right paw off the ground.

She didn't seem in pain as I sat her in the back of our car, though I tried to get her to lie down, pressing her backside down lightly to keep pressure off her paw. She wanted nothing to do with that, instead taking her position between the two front seats, only this time holding one leg off the console.

The veterinarian was only a mile away, and was easy enough to find. When we walked in, a 20-something year old nurse acted like she was expecting us, and brought us straight into an examination room. "Awww, Mr. Tubbs said you'd be coming. Let's take a look at the paw."

Bahama winced as the nurse lifted up the paw and squeezed it, but didn't let that stop her from licking the face of the nurse, who didn't seem to mind.

"Yeah, seems like something is a little off. Dr. Sutton will be right in."

Bahama wanted to jump off the metal examination table, but I held her in place. After a few minutes, Dr. Sutton walked in.

After shaking my hand and introducing himself, he put on gloves and checked her heart rate and temperature. Bahama didn't like that much, especially the second half, and temporarily forgot she had a hurt leg.

"Easy there girl. Her heart rate is up a little, but her temperature is fine, so I don't think there is a break, as that can raise the temperature some. Do you mind if we take some x-rays just in case?"

Dr. Sutton lifted Bahama and took her to the back, and I sat down on a chair in the office. I was overcome with thoughts as it occurred to me that this is what my wife had done for a living for so many years. I had never seen her work, but I always imagined her calm and understanding when it came to her job, mainly because that's how she was in everyday life.

"Looks like it's just a strain. With a few days of rest she should be okay. We'll go ahead and wrap it up, keeping it in place, which should relieve some of her pain. She probably won't like the tape, but I'd like to try to keep it on her for at least two weeks. We'll also give you a low dose pain medicine. The pain will get worse for her as the day goes on, so you can probably just get away with giving it to her at night before you go to sleep. Do you have any questions?"

"Nope, just glad it wasn't worse. Thank you for seeing us on such short notice."

"Oh, we'd do anything for Bruce around here; he's one of our favorite patients," he said with a laugh. Thinking about Bruce's woeful look after his mishap with Bahama, I imagined him having a hard time at the vet, so I wondered if Dr. Sutton was being facetious with his last statement. He then added, "The nurse will be right in with the medicine and the bill."

She came right in, and I was surprised to see the bill was nearly $400 bucks, but I reasoned it was to be expected because of the x-rays and seeing us on short notice. Additionally, I had no idea of the price of animal care in Vegas.

When I handed the receptionist the bill and

reached for my wallet with the other she stopped me. "I guess the nurse didn't tell you. Mr. Tubbs told us he'll take care of the bill. He felt so bad."

"Wow, that's so nice of him. Can you please tell him that I said that next time you see him?"

I had saved about 400 dollars today. That should be plenty enough for ordering delivery when Jen got to my apartment less than an hour from when we left the vet.

29

I made Bahama a makeshift doggy bed on the carpet, but of course she wasted no time hopping over to the bed, three legged, and jumping up. I myself hopped into the shower, two legged, and washed quickly, shaved, and dressed. Even at my own house I retained my fear of being late, but even after all my worrying, I still had 15 minutes to go before Jen was scheduled to arrive. I waited at the computer, briefly considering looking up menus of local delivery joints, but hadn't yet decided if I was ready to eat in front of Jen yet, so instead just sat there.

At about two minutes after 8:00 she arrived. After giving me a hug, a hug I was learning to enjoy more and more, she walked in and saw Bahama. Bahama had sat up but was stuck in an inner battle on whether or not to jump down from the bed, concerned it would hurt her paw. Jen, seeing her dilemma, walked over to Bahama for their first introduction.

"Awww what happened to you little girl," while looking back up to me. "You didn't tell me she had hurt herself. What happened?"

"She had a little mishap at the dog park today with a dog three times her size."

"Uh oh! I guess she's okay since she's home already?"

"Yes, Bruce's owner was very apologetic and even footed the bill. It's just a sprain; she should be back to her old self in a few days," I told her.

"I sure hope so. I know she's your traveling partner – can't split up the dynamic duo!"

"Only thing is I probably shouldn't go out tonight because we were told she should rest her leg for a few days," I said slightly hesitantly because I really didn't want her to leave.

"Oh. No. I'm easy, I don't mind hanging out if you don't mind me hanging around." I certainly didn't mind. She continued, "Are you hungry? I'm starving. Want to get some Chinese?" she asked as she kicked off her shoes. She was dressed in a light sweater and jeans, so she wasn't necessarily dressed out for a big night on the town, relieving some of my worry that she had bigger plans.

"Yes, I'm starving," I said, continuing to tell silly white lies out of nervousness, "you got a favorite place?"

"No, I'm not too familiar with Henderson, but you can just do an internet search for Chinese food in Henderson and take your pick. Don't they all taste the same anyway?"

We ordered food, and while waiting it dawned on me that this was most likely my night to spill my guts, as Jen had done so on our previous date. Even when I just thought about it to myself it was hard for me to use the word "date" so I usually just glided over that word in my brain. Still, even though I had been out of the game for over ten years I knew that this was considered a date and it was time for me to do some talking.

Over orange and sesame chicken, I opened up. Even during our conversation I wondered if I was talking because I was afraid of the silence.

I told her about how my wife had been had been my first love. I told her most of the same story I had relived in my drive across country. I told her everything from meeting in college that first day to the day she died, though I left out some details about the end of her life. I did this because not only was it hard for me to talk about but also because a lot of those conversations I had with my wife – the sharing of fears and things we'll miss out together once she died – were sacred to me.

Like my last date with Jen, time seemed to go quicker when we were together. When I was done talking about my wife, for the most part, we sat in silence for a few minutes, Jen loving on Bahama and I left in my thoughts. She finally broke the silence.

"Have you had a chance to see more of Vegas?" I realized that a lot of what I had said was pretty heavy, and maybe she thought this was a safer topic for now. I couldn't really blame her.

"The truth is," and it was the truth, "I haven't done many Vegasy things since I've been here. Most of the time I have been hanging out in the room with Bahama and attempting to write. Oh, and eating too much. That Fatburger is pretty good," I added with a laugh that I had adopted from my date.

"Don't take this next question the wrong way, but why are you here?"

I thought for a second, then explained to her that after just sitting in the house for a full year and reading stories about people who have gone all over the world I felt like Vegas was one of the "must see places," and yes, I did the air quotation marks.

After another moment I added, "I think I got really comfortable in the Keys. I dare say I almost felt at home there. Sure, there were thousands of tourists pouring in and out of there every day, but when I was there I didn't feel like I was one of them. At least after a week or so, anyway. Heck, I even got a job there."

"Vegas is a little different, huh?"

"Yeah, I'm thinking I came here just for the hell of it without thinking too much of why I was going. I'm an old man, I guess, I don't have a huge desire to go around clubs and bar hopping anymore," I fought the urge to say "unless you were there."

"Well, if you were up for it, I could take you back to my stomping grounds and see how you like that."

I knew she was talking about her trips to the Pacific Coast, but couldn't help it.

"Eh, I don't know, what exactly is there for me to see in Kansas City? A tornado? No thanks."

Jen leaned over just far enough from the bed she was sitting and temporarily stopped rubbing on Bahama's belly to punch me in the arm. "You know what I mean!"

Jen left a little while later after that, saying Bahama needed to get some rest. We made plans to get together soon after.

This time when she came in for a hug she planted a kiss on my cheek. It wasn't a friendly smooch. I was taken aback, not because I didn't like it, which I did, but because it was the first time I had even had those types of thoughts for over two years. She caught my eye to see my reaction, but because I recoiled a bit she believed I wasn't interested. She went back in for a hug, which I gladly accepted and left me with a smile.

As I drifted off to sleep that night I only hoped I hadn't disappointed her.

30

We started seeing each other a few times a week, and I suspected we both wished it could be even more, but her work schedule prevented that. In general we'd check out a restaurant or bar, and end up talking for hours. On almost all of our dates she would ask me what I had been up to since our last date, knowing I had done nothing "Vegasy." After a few dates and me answering this question with my typical "Oh, you know, stayed in the room and wrote and hung out with Bahama," I knew she was teasing me. Around the sixth or seventh time we had agreed to go on a date, she called me a few hours before to tell me that we're doing something "Vegasy" that night.

"Oh really, what exactly are we doing?" I asked, thinking it was going to be gambling or a show.

"I'm taking you to a strip club!"

"Ummm," was about all I could say.

"I have a friend who is a bartender there, not a stripper, and we can sit and talk with her. Don't judge it before you try it; you'll have a good time."

I was surprised she thought this is something I would like to do, and even wondered if she had hidden alternatives as to why she was dating me. But I also figured she was going through a lot of work if she was planning on scamming me in any way, so I tossed these thoughts to the side. I still hadn't talked. After a few more seconds, she spoke again.

"Listen, if you really don't want to go that's fine. I don't want to force you. I just thought for someone who seems to enjoy a lot of experiences you would get a kick out of this. Maybe it will even end up in your writing one day! Trust me, it's not my intention to make you feel uncomfortable, and if you don't want to go, no hard feelings at all. "

I apprehensively agreed despite remembering my last time at a strip club for my 21st birthday. After a while of sitting in the room and contemplating the plans we had set for the evening, I did come to the conclusion that it would indeed be a break from the normal for me. It may have been an odd way of showing it, but I could tell Jen was certainly looking out for my best interests.

We got to Tigris a little after nine o'clock. Being that it was a Thursday the strip club wasn't packed, but it was busy enough that I didn't think it would be considered a slow night in the strip club world. When you walked into Tigris there were bathrooms to the right, and everything else was to the left. The place was huge, and seemed to go farther than the naked eye could see, but that could have been from the fog machines they implemented during their shows. Upon entering, you first came to the bar, located on the left side of the room. If you continued walking straight to the other wall you would pass multiple stages with different kinds of set-ups. The last stage you came to was for the headliner acts, as it had the biggest stage, with a long cat-walk, and the most stage-side seating. On a Thursday night though, all of the action ended before the main stage.

Jen stopped at the bar and asked for her friend Ashley, who was on a smoke break, as there is a no inside smoking in Vegas. After ordering a couple of drinks from the other bartender, Ashley came back in. Jen had explained to me in the car that she had met Ashley at Burger Bar when Ashley had been on a date. In much the same way I may have misjudged Jen when I first met her, there was more to Ashley than just being a bartender in a strip club. She had left Chicago after working as a legal secretary for a popular and important law firm. After a few years of that work she burned out, and came to Vegas for a change of scenery. Lots of people doing that lately, it seemed.

Ashley introduced herself with a strong handshake, one I imagined that came from bartending, as Jen had a similar grip. Ashley had blonde hair, a nose piercing, and very large breasts which I'm sure would have gotten her another job within Tigris had she wanted it. Ashley was busy, but between customers she and Jen talked and caught up, not having seen each other for a few months due to conflicting work schedules. Jen had introduced me as "her friend Mike" and Ashley cocked an eyebrow towards Jen, as in asking "is he just 'your friend Mike' or is he more?" I'm not sure how I expected Jen to introduce me, but you can bet I thought about it the remainder of the night. This was an especially hard thought to stay focused on when you think the girl next to you may be your girlfriend and you are surrounded by a bunch of gorgeous naked women.

Female patrons get a lot of attention in a strip club. While Jen was there mostly to show me a good time and to catch up with a friend, she did her best to make her fellow peers in the service industry feel wanted by giving the talent a good tip, though all she did was talk to most of the strippers, opting out of a free show or dance.

I had a clear shot from my barstool to the closest stage, and spent most of the night peeking out towards that when Jen and Ashley were in conversation. It wasn't that they weren't involving me, but with the music as loud as it as it was, it was hard to have a two way conversation, let alone a three-way. Conversation.

A bachelor party was taking place, and at one point they took the groom-to-be onto the stage and sat him on a chair with his hands tied behind his back and around the stripper pole. Flashbacks of my 21st birthday ran rampant.

Shortly after the future groom was tied up, a woman was on his lap, giving him a lap dance. But then she called two of her friends over, and at one point they were all on him. His buddies, who had surely spent a lot of money to make his friend the center of attention, were all loving it, but I thought I saw an uncomfortable look on their tied up friend. The original stripper then did this move where she jumped to the top of the stripper pole, and slid down head first, ending with her head in the man's lap and her legs wrapped securely around his head. When she gyrated I swore you could hear his head clank off the pole. When the two songs were over, the man tried his best to smile, but he basically leaped off the stage back into the comfort of the private booth on the other side of the stage.

Shortly after that show, Jen went outside with Ashley when she went outside for another smoke break. I also figured this is when Jen would tell Ashley about our relationship. I didn't have much time to ponder what exactly she would say to her friend, as a few seconds after Jen was out of the bar, a long-legged stripper sat next to me on Jen's barstool.

"Hey, I'm Misty, is that your girlfriend?" she asked while extending her hand limply for a handshake. After the handshake her hand landed on my thigh, and stayed there. I contemplated my answers, as I didn't think me telling Misty that Jen was my girlfriend would deter her in the slightest. However, I didn't want to put Jen in any possible embarrassing situations, so I elected to keep her out of it.

"No, we're just friends. She's just showing me around," I said, with my nervous laughter creeping back in.

"I was hoping you'd say that. I think you're really cute, do you want a private dance?"

"I'm really sorry, I have no money on me," I told her. I even reached into my pockets to flip them inside out for emphasis. My wallet was in my back pocket, but she didn't need to know that. I fully expected that move and line would cause her to get up and move on to the next guy, but it didn't

"That's cool, baby. Do you mind if we just sit and talk for a while?"

"No," I figured she could have been tired from a night full of grinding and wearing ridiculously tall heels, so if she needed to use me to take a rest, I figured it was the least I could do.

"I really do think you're cute, you know. If she isn't your girlfriend, like you say, I wouldn't mind going out with you. I don't plan on being a stripper forever and you look like as nice a guy as there is in here. I haven't even seen you get a dance yet, so chances are you aren't a creep either."

I didn't know what to say, so I semi-lied, "I'm just getting over a tough relationship." While that was true I was really just thinking about Jen and wondering when she was going to come back in and save me from this situation. I also thought that Jen coming back could be a cause for concern. I know Jen wouldn't care I was talking to a stripper, knowing she most likely approached me, but it could make for some odd questioning based on the lines I had fed Misty so far.

"That's very nice of you to say, and I don't mind

your choice of profession; I'm just not interested in a relationship right now. It's nothing against you."

Seemingly ignoring my statement, she asked, "Do you like art? I used to love going to art museums. I used to want to be an artist."

"Um. I don't know much about it, but I appreciate certain works of art." Like my date for the evening.

For the next ten minutes she told me about her favorite works of art, and was fascinated to hear I was a writer, an artist in my own right, she told me. Unfortunately, the things I had written weren't quite as fascinating to her.

I then saw Ashley back behind the bar. I wondered where Jen was. I looked over Misty's shoulder towards the entrance to see her leaning against the wall flashing me a smile that was more of a smirk. She had wanted me to have a "Vegasy" experience and I guess talking to a depressed stripper about art fit the bill.

"I'm really sorry that you aren't interested, I think we would have had a good time. I better get back to work. Thanks for your time, love." As she got up, her hand brushed way up my thigh, surely by design.

"You should start painting again," was all I could think to say as she walked back towards the stage.

She turned around with a smile and said, "I'll think about it," before slipping out of her slinky dress and climbing the stairs to get on the stage.

Jen came back and said, "I see you made a friend," while pushing her stool closer to mine and laying her hand on my thigh, mimicking the behavior of Misty. She may have been joking, but I was much happier with Jen's hand on my thigh than Misty's. When Jen left her hand there, I wasn't complaining.

After telling Jen about my conversation with

Misty, she asked if I was ready to go. I said I thought that was for the best, as I made a look towards Misty.

Jen said goodbye to Ashley and made customary plans to "see you again soon." Ashley smiled a knowing smile at me. I nodded at her, and heading out the door, Jen leading me by the hand.

On our way out Misty, having just finished her dance routine, caught my eye from the other side of the bar and said, "I thought you said she wasn't your girlfriend," but her smile didn't suggest she was particularly mad at this development.

"I guess I got lucky," was all I could think to say to her, feeling embarrassed that I had lied to my new stripper friend.

"Yeah, yeah," was all she said as she turned her attention back to her new friend, an older gentleman at the bar who seemed a lot more interested in her than I had been.

I am lucky, I thought, as Jen whisked me out of the door.

31

When we got in my car I asked her what she wanted to do next. It was still fairly early, at least by Vegas standards. I told her I didn't really know what to do, and that she was the expert.

"You want to come back to my place?"

This was a surprise because she had never asked if I wanted to go to her place before, nor have I ever asked. I had picked her up and dropped her off at her house before, but never invited myself in.

"Sure, that sounds good."

We pulled up to her high-rise apartment building just a block off The Strip about ten minutes later. I drove to where I was used to picking her up, but she told me to swing around to the opposite side and let the valet take care of it. This was the first time I would ever be going to someone's house that had valet. I thought that was cool, but decided not to bring that up as I learning those things were expected in Vegas.

I was nervous about going up to her apartment because I wasn't sure what she had in mind. I even secretly wondered if her trip to the strip club had turned her on. Or maybe even Jen seeing me with another woman, even if it was a stripper, had made her a bit jealous. A million thoughts crossed my mind as we entered the elevator.

"What, no elevator man?" I asked jokingly.

"Nope, the valet is going to have to be good enough. Oh, and 24 hour security. Also, there is tennis on the roof if you want to get a set in?" Apparently she had picked up that I was both impressed and surprised about the valet.

We walked in and her apartment was gorgeous. The layout was a square, which included a kitchen with a bar on one side, and a small electric fireplace in another corner. Everything in the apartment was very contemporary and sleek. Her television was in a built-in entertainment unit that included bookshelves that were filled to the brim. In front of the books were pictures of what I suspected to be members of her family.

"Would you like a drink?" she asked, as I was getting a closer look at the photos.

"Sure, thanks. I'll have whatever you are having."

While she went to make the drinks I looked at the pictures on the bookshelf. I noticed an older couple that had to be her parents because they looked just like her, especially her mom. I could see that she got her looks from her mom as well. Her frame came from her dad who was thin, but appeared to be muscular. On another shelf was a group shot of a family on a big wrap-around porch in front of a big house.

Jen brought our drinks and sat on the couch, kicking off her shoes in the process. I sat next to her and she snuggled closer.

"Did you have a good time tonight?" she asked.

She smelled amazing, or the apartment smelled amazing. I hadn't noticed this in the car.

"Yeah, I made a new friend and got to hang out with you," I said, laughing.

"Well, I was just hoping to give you a real Vegas experience before you move on to the next town."

I wanted to tell her that as long as she was around I wouldn't be too eager to "move on to the next town," but instead said, "I thank you for that," while setting my drink down on her glass coffee table.

I think she was waiting for me to do that, because

in almost the same instant, she set down her glass and moved even closer to me in one motion. She nestled her head under my neck. I thought she was just going to stay there, but then she kissed my neck. I recoiled slightly, which I hoped she didn't notice because like her kiss on my cheek in my doorway a few weeks before. I was enjoying it, despite my natural response.

"Is this okay?" she asked.

"Yes," I said, though I didn't know if I was telling the truth.

She kissed me up my neck and onto my lips, our first kiss. At first I was hesitant, a million thoughts running through my head, among other places, but I kissed her back. After a few minutes of this she began to unbutton my shirt and swung her leg over me and sat on my lap. At this I began to freak out.

In my head, I wanted to just gently place her back on the couch, but instead I was a little more forceful than I had anticipated. After apologizing for nearly throwing her on the floor, I spoke again.

"I'm really sorry, I can't do this, it's just that I've never..."

"It's okay, you don't have to explain." I saw some disappointment in her eyes, but she also gave me her smile that seemed to tell me that it was okay, or at least, will be. After a few tense moments, neither of us knowing what to say or do next, I spoke.

"I really like you. I mean really, really like you, but I'm just not ready yet. I know my problem is more than tonight, but tonight has been so weird for me too that this doesn't feel right. An hour ago I was at a strip club and now I'm here with you and..."

"I understand. I'm sorry; we don't have to do anything."

The last thing I wanted her to do was feel like she had to apologize, which led me to apologize. After a few more minutes of awkward apologies I figured it was best if I just left.

"I still want to see you again if that's okay." I don't know why I said that but I felt like I was pleading with her to give me another chance without actually saying those words.

"I would certainly hope so. I want to see you again soon."

Her words instantly made me feel better. Her look was sincere. While I knew this would probably be a setback in our relationship, I felt relieved it wouldn't be an ending to our relationship.

As I headed home, I thought in my head that the only woman I had slept with other than my wife my entire adult life was Bahama. That thought started off as a joke in my head but slowly turned into dread. I literally said out loud to the empty car, "Yeah and it will stay like that if you aren't careful."

32

After another night in the loving paws of Bahama, I woke up to face the day. I didn't sleep well that night, contemplating the call I would have to make. Around the time the sun started going up I finally fell asleep. I had dreams about Jen kissing me. Usually this would have been a great way to spend the day sleeping, but all the dreams ended with me throwing Jen off me, and in a particularly interesting sequence, with my wife breaking through the wall, Kool-Aid Man style, wondering exactly what was going on. I woke up before I could explain.

There would be no art conversations with strippers today, as I decided I would put in a good writing day, or at least try. I found multiple excuses to keep me from writing. I always seem to let more serious matters marinate in my brain for a day, a month, a year, or even two.

Late in the day I had thought about calling Jen, but conveniently put it off long enough to know that she would be at work. I had hoped she would call me, but it was for the better she didn't because I didn't know what to say if she had called. The next day was Saturday, and I knew she would be off the whole day, so I told myself if she didn't call by a certain hour I would call her.

Fortunately for my nerves I didn't have to spend the entire day wondering what I was going to say to Jen when I called. Around 9 a.m. while still lying in bed, my phone rang. It was Jen. After a sleepy hello from me, Jen began talking.

"I want to apologize for the other night. I probably came on a little strong, and I should have asked you more about how you were feeling. I also shouldn't have come onto you just after leaving a strip club, but I have to let you know that I would have done that no matter what we had done that night. I wasn't trying to take advantage of you, but if I came off like that I'm truly sorry."

I was still waking up so it took an extra second to comprehend everything she was saying, so I decided to start with what came most simply to me, for my sake – something I should have said a couple nights ago before leaving.

"I never want you to think that you have to apologize for that, or anything else. I'm flattered that you would want to spend time with me like that." After a few moments of pause I figured she expected me to keep talking, so I did.

"I have to admit that hanging out at a strip club and then going back to your house and making out had crossed my mind as an interesting choice of timing and that may have contributed to me freaking out a bit , but I should have known, and I do know, that you aren't like that." When she continued to be quiet on the other end, I spoke again, not knowing exactly what she wanted to hear, but began thinking I had a good idea.

"I wish I was telling you this in person, but here it goes. I really loved my wife; she was the only girl – woman – I ever loved. Now everything I do with a woman – you – I only have to compare to my wife. I know I shouldn't think like that, but it's what I've been struggling with as I get to know you. In many ways, many of the things I've been doing with you are like I'm doing them for the very first time. I also know that I really like you and that if I want to continue seeing you and getting to know you that I can't keep comparing everything happening now with everything that once was."

After another moment, she finally spoke, the tears coming through. "I'm coming over, is that okay?"

"Of course."

When she arrived about 20 minutes later, giving me just enough time to bathe and rid myself of morning breath, she walked in. I could tell she had been crying, but it appeared to be lightly, and not a heavy sob.

"Are you okay?"

She hugged me, and didn't let go for a while. When she let go she kept holding onto my hands, and said "You're so sweet. I never expect you to stop loving your wife, and I would find it weird if you did. If you could find a way to give me a piece of your heart next to her I would like that very much."

I leaned into her, and kissed her. I remember thinking that in a perfect world this is what our first kiss would have been like, but quickly tossed aside that idea. No, this was perfect regardless of which kiss it was.

For the first time in my life, I took the initiative with a woman. From our standing position we moved closer to the bed, and I laid us down gently. At first Bahama thought this was a game that she hadn't been invited to, but after a few more minutes of neither of us paying attention to her, she got the drift, sulking off the bed and on to her makeshift bed on the floor.

The next half an hour or so, time was a blur, but a blur of pure ecstasy. I remember hoping I was doing well, but not really caring because I was enjoying the moment too much to let my mind get wrapped up in the details. When we finished I did something I remember only seeing in the movies and wondering how they ever did that. I rolled over and fell asleep.

When I woke up I was instantly embarrassed that

I had fallen asleep and was going to say something to that effect, but when I rolled over Jen was gone. I had thought she had left, and began feeling a mix between anger and bewilderment. It was the first time I had ever made love with someone other than my wife, and she knew that and was just going to leave? Before I could work myself up too much, I heard her speak.

"You really loved her, huh?" She was at my desk in front of my computer. She spoke again.

"I hope you don't mind, you had this up and I just started reading it. You are an amazing writer. Is this a book?"

In my past I had hardly let anybody read what I wrote, but for some reason this didn't anger me. Perhaps I was still relieved she hadn't left.

"Those are just things I'm trying to write to remember her memory. I waited too long and some of it has slipped away, but I couldn't have done it any sooner. Every time I tried I could never get anything out without getting too emotional." Jen smiled at me, but before she said anything I said in a joking tone, "My journal is on there too if you want to read it. There's some interesting stuff about you in there."

"Oh really, I might just do that," she said after faking like she was going to look it up before getting out of the chair, wearing nothing but my New River University t-shirt, and jumping into the bed with me. For the rest of the day we took turns spilling our guts to each other, among other things. I had felt that she had told me more about herself, so I thought it only fair to tell her more about myself. I knew she had read a lot of the writings I had done about my wife, but went into even more detail.

At the end of the day I told Jen how thankful I was to get to know her. I told her that I couldn't imagine there were too many people in the world that would have a relationship with someone who talked about their past so much. I told her about my attempts at visiting a therapist after my wife died, but that it wasn't for me. I told Jen that her kind of therapy was definitely more for me, and I knew I was lucky to have her in my life. Finally, I told her I hoped I wasn't talking about my past too much.

"I love hearing about your past. It's really refreshing to hear about a couple that made it work when so many don't nowadays. I know you are a good man by what you tell me about your past. I will tell you if you are ever talking about it too much."

After contemplating in silence for a while – a silence I was comfortable with for the first time in a while – Jen asked, "Do you mind if I stay the night?" I answered a little quickly, "No, of course not," which caused Jen to smile and roll over closer to me. This turned out to be another night I didn't get too much sleep.

33

The next morning we got out of bed and headed down to the lobby of my complex for the continental breakfast. I had expected light talking to join us with our light breakfast, but I was mistaken.

"I have something to tell you, but before I do I don't want you to think this was some big plan of mine, the last few nights. Especially last night."

"Um, okay, what is it?" As you can imagine a million possibilities went through my head. I somehow went to the thought that she somehow knew she was pregnant already, but I also realized that would have been some kind of record between what we did and finding out she was expecting. Still, I'm sure the color drained from my face.

"You know the girl that's been training at Burger Bar I told you about? She's taking my place. My last day is next week."

I was silent, processing everything for a minute or two. My first thought was wondering what she was going to do next, so that's what I asked.

"What are you going to do next?"

"I had been thinking of leaving Vegas for a while. In fact, the night of our first date was when I originally put in my notice that I was leaving. I told them that since I didn't exactly have to be anywhere by a certain date that I could stick around until they found someone to replace me. When we went on our first date – and I'm sure you understand – I didn't think it would turn into this, something so great." When she finished she took a deep breath, appearing anxious to hear my response.

"I can understand that, I'd be lying if I told you I

thought we would become this. If you knew my track record with women, especially lately, I wasn't exactly holding out hope for a great relationship either."

I then continued after a few seconds, "Where are you planning to go?"

"Before you and I got serious I thought I would go back to Kansas City, but after meeting you, you inspired me to keep going with my travels. I know at some point I have to think about settling down and getting a real job again, and in my mind I've just felt like this is the right time. I'm over 30 years old."

"Now that we both appear more serious than we originally thought, what do you want to do?" I asked, while nudging in closer to her.

"I don't know, but I know that I want to experience things with you. Correct me if I'm wrong, but I don't think you love Vegas. When you talk about the Keys I can hear it in your voice how much you enjoyed it. I have some places I'd like to go with you too and see if we can find places we like together."

Over a plate of shared danishes, I hoped I showed that I wanted to be with her too, sealing my answer with a kiss. She didn't have to say another word. I knew she wanted to be with me too.

"So, are you ready to leave Vegas?" she asked.

34

"In what I've come to describe as the last part of my journey, I decided to come visit you. I haven't been here since the day you were buried. It rained this morning, but now it's warm. You always thought it was funny that I liked the rain so much. While you would run into the store from the parking lot I always took my time. Then again, you said I took my time doing almost everything, including visiting you for the first time today.

"I always felt guilty that I wasn't coming by to just sit at your gravestone to spend time with you and talk to you. But I always justified my reason for not visiting in two ways. The first reason, I told myself I wasn't going to visit you, is because for a full year after you died I didn't do anything that I thought you would be interested in. That can also be thought of as I didn't do anything that I was proud of telling you.

"The second reason was because I had a strong feeling that you were always with me. I'm sure I may have used this reasoning to justify not seeing you, but I really did think you were there. When I was gearing up to go on my journey, one small step at a time, I felt you were both there to get me going in the right direction, but also telling me there was no rush. When you are under distress like I was for quite a long time you wonder what is real and what isn't, but I really did feel your presence, even in the darkest of times.

"Of course, what's most likely the real reason I didn't come visit you is because I was scared. I was scared about how it would make me feel. I was scared of what I would say to you, or if I would say anything at all. Most of all I was scared that the memories we shared would all come flooding back to me. While in theory that should have made me feel happy, at the time of my mourning I just thought I would regress from any progress I had made. I realized now that there was no right or wrong answer.

"When I took my trip it was with you in mind, of course. At first, everything I did new was met with the thought that it was something I would never get to do with you. Many times I just thought about going back home, lying in bed for another year, or longer, and relying on my parents to take care of me. But I kept going. I owed it to you.

"It's clear you were there every step of the way. While you were living you always wanted me to reconnect with my sister. You knew how close Chloe and I were growing up, and you always pushed me to make the first call, or first visit, but I didn't. Well, when I got in the car the first day of the journey, you not only pointed me south, but you pointed me to Chloe and her beautiful daughter Cassidy. I see signs of you in her, including her love of animals. She's only seven, but she has already told me several times she wants to be a veterinarian. As my trip progressed I believe I never would have taken that first step in reconciling with my sister if it wasn't for you.

"The Keys. I couldn't figure out if you directed me there. We had never really talked about that part of the country, but during my many hours of traveling I think I figured it out. You knew I always had this desire to 'do something different.' You told me many times that I was already following the path less traveled because I was a writer, but we both knew I meant something else. In Florida, I worked on a fishing boat. That was certainly different. Also, just the town of Key West is different. I love it there, but after a few weeks, I start to long for something else.

"I think that longing was the wanting to come home again. You always said I was a homebody, but I always seemed to want to prove to you, and more likely myself, that I wasn't. So instead of going home during my trip I went to the most opposite place I could think of, Las Vegas. As I suspected, and I'm sure you probably tried to give me signs, I didn't like Vegas too much, but I'm sure glad I went there. I was on the road well over a year, seeing just about every part of the country worth seeing and meeting great people along the way. They, whoever they are, say you can't go home again, but here I am, and I don't have any more plans on leaving anytime soon.

"Life sure is different without you, and we all miss you every day. Bahama is doing well, and enjoyed our trip as much as I did, if not more. If anything, she sure ate well. She is happy to be back home. Like me, she always sleeps much better in her own bed, which is of course also my bed.

"I'm still writing, and that's a big reason why I'm here today. A couple of months before I headed out on my journey I started writing again. I tried to keep a journal, but often times too many memories would come back and I would set it aside for weeks before writing another entry. I also didn't have much to write about.

"When I started my trip, I didn't really intend to make writing a daily thing, but as the trip progressed that's exactly what happened. I would say that when I became comfortable in the Keys I began writing every day, even if for just 10 or 15 minutes.

"Those writings, with the support and encouragement of loved ones, became the copy of the book I'm leaving with you today, though I have a feeling you have already read it. I hope you like it. Everything in it was written with you in mind, and in honor of you. I love you, and I always will."

As I finished up the letter, Cassidy called from the limo, "Hurry up, Uncle Mike! You don't want to keep Jen waiting, do you?"

She was right. I certainly didn't want to keep my bride waiting on our wedding day.

Acknowledgements

While I agree writing is a singular pursuit, the construction of a book is not. With that, I have many people to thank.

Thank you to Mike Reed for creating an amazing cover. Without a cover, there would be no book.

Thank you to my cousin, Jessica Woods, for going through a red marker (or three) while editing the first copy of my book.

Thank you to my step-mother, Annette Jones, for also adding valuable input in the editing process.

Thank you to Jeremy Congdon and his team at Immerge Technologies for creating my website: **www.rwjonesauthor.com**.

Thank you to Nathan Gottlieb for helping me through the many ups and downs associated with writing a book.

Thank you to Marianne Jones for being the first person to read this book as a book.

Thank you to my friends and family who supported and motivated me throughout the entire process.

Thank you to my wife, Jessica, for taking care of all the other things that were over my head during the writing process, including putting this acknowledgements page in the correct place before publication.

About the Author

R.W. Jones is a former freelance writer with a passion for reading, writing, and traveling. His career has allowed him to cover numerous sporting events and interview some of the biggest names in sports. He currently lives in Virginia with his wife, their dog Kokomo and cat Charlotte. Check out more on R.W. Jones at his website **www.rwjonesauthor.com**.